T0113382

Christian Beliefs

by

J. Deotis Roberts

A J. Deotis Roberts Press Publication

Third Edition
June 2000

Published by:
The J. Deotis Roberts Press
Post Office Box 10127
Silver Spring, MD 20914

ISBN 978-0-9674601-5-4

LCCN 00-190049

Printed in the United States by
Morris Publishing
3212 East Highway 30
Kearney, NE 68847
1-800-650-7888

Dedication

This primer of Christian belief has resulted from years of dialogue and study. I dedicate it to my many theological students at Howard Divinity School, Eastern Baptist Theological Seminary, Yale Divinity School and Duke Divinity School

Table of Contents

i	Author's Note
ii	Preface for 1st and 2nd Editions
v	Preface for the 2000 Edition

PART I
FOUNDATIONS

1	Chapter 1	The Bible as Source Book
5	Chapter 2	The Living Word
9	Chapter 3	The Living Bible: The Old Testament
14	Chapter 4	The Living Bible: The New Testament
21	Chapter 5	The Living Tradition

PART II
CHRISTIAN BELIEFS INTERPRETED

29	Chapter 6	The Existence of God
32	Chapter 7	God as Personal Spirit
35	Chapter 8	The Holiness of God
38	Chapter 9	The Righteousness of God
42	Chapter 10	The Love of God
45	Chapter 11	The Tri-Unity of God
49	Chapter 12	What Does It Mean To Be Human?
53	Chapter 13	Sin as a Universal Reality
57	Chapter 14	What Will You Do With Jesus?
60	Chapter 15	"What Think Ye of Christ?"
64	Chapter 16	The Coming of Christ
67	Chapter 17	Ring In The Christ That Is To Be
71	Chapter 18	The Easter Message Today
74	Chapter 19	The Holy Spirit and Sanctification
79	Chapter 20	Grace and Sanctification
83	Chapter 21	The People of God
87	Chapter 22	Bread and Wine and Water
92	Chapter 23	The Christian Lifestyle

96 Chapter 24 "In The End, God!"
100 Chapter 25 Conclusion

---

103 *Christian Beliefs* Guidance
148 Special Books

Author's Note

Inclusive Language

While, as author, I have made a serious attempt to use inclusive language, I have not been completely successful. It has not been too difficult to overcome sexist language when dealing with purely human concerns. Even there, however, the grammar seems awkward but reasonably appropriate. I have been reluctant to tamper with biblical and theological language and concepts for the sake of historic meanings. I am prepared to admit the patriarchal bent of this tradition. I prefer to exercise the care and cautious reflection before exercising further liberty regarding this matter. I approach this concern with both openness and caution.

Bible Translations

Unless otherwise indicated, all biblical references are taken from *The Holy Bible*, King James Version. Other references are from the Revised Standard Version of the Bible (RSV) copyrighted 1946, 1952, 1971 and 1973 by the Division of Christian Education of the National Council of Churches of Christ in the USA, and the New English Bible (NEB), copyrighted 1961 and 1970 by the Delegates of the Oxford University Press and the Syndics of the Cambridge University Press. Used by permission.

Preface

The first edition of *Christian Beliefs* resulted from a request made by the Christian Education Department of the Mount Carmel Baptist Church in Washington, DC. The late Rev. R.L. Patterson, pastor of this historic church, gave me his loyal support and wrote the foreword to the first edition. It was a privilege to work with this outstanding congregation that has placed so much emphasis upon education within its membership. This dialogue with laity enabled me to state with greater simplicity and clarity the materials that I had shared with seminarians at the Howard Divinity School.

The work has been widely received and used by a variety of individuals and groups on campuses and in churches. Recently, I had the privilege of sharing theological insights with the Office of Evangelism of the American Baptist Churches in the USA. Dr. Duncan McIntosh, of this distinguished staff, read *Christian Beliefs*, introduced it to the staff, and together they requested that a revision of this work be prepared primarily for their use. This will make it useful to an even wider audience than before. The suggestions that this team have made have enriched the text immensely and have made it much more valuable as a resource on the essential affirmations of the Christian faith.

The book is one that takes seriously the authority of the Bible. While I am by specialization a systematic and philosophical theologian, this work is essentially biblical theology. I am deeply grateful that the leadership at Mount Carmel and the American Baptist Churches in the USA has inspired my careful look at Scripture as a basis for theological reflection. This has been an incentive for personal enrichment as well as a challenge to share my growth with others. As a result, my total theological outlook has become more biblical. This later edition should reflect the fruits of the search in Scripture that has intervened between the editions.

Another characteristic of the book is its Christological focus. In an informal conversation, Dr. McIntosh observed that a book of this type could be theological without being Chistological. He went on to assert that *Christian Beliefs* is both. He indicated that this Christological bias of the book had a special appeal to him and his staff. As I read and reread the original text, the significance of this profound observation became clear. It dawned on me that my personal credo has taken shape as I wrote with others, as well as myself, in mind. The reader should study this text with both an "I believe" and a "we believe" emphasis. But whether we read it for personal spiritual growth or growth in fellowship with others, I believe that it will be especially helpful to remember its avowedly Christological focus.

Another aspect of this work is noteworthy. *Christian Beliefs* is evangelical in tone. Theologically speaking, it is soteriological . It takes seriously the reality of sin and evil in the human and cosmic orders. But it treats, at the same time, the grace and forgiveness of God. *Christian Beliefs* expresses, in light of faith affirmations, an awareness of social sins as well as personal sins. The human part in salvation is stated without toning down God's saving work through Christ and the Holy Spirit. At the heart of the discussion is both the need and the provision for salvation.

Finally, we will point out the ecumenical dimension of *Christian Beliefs*. It goes to the heart of the historic faith of Christians without being intolerant of those who may differ on points of doctrine. It raises the essential aspects of the faith of Christians in such a way that all who confess this faith will be challenged to seek a deeper understanding and commitment concerning their beliefs. Certainly a book of this type may do more, but it should not do less. There are other things that we might say concerning our intention and/or achievement here.

Suffice it to say, however, that *Christian Beliefs* is biblical, Christological, soteriological and ecumenical.

In Part I, we present what we call "Foundations". It is clear that the grounding of this volume is securely in Scripture. Part II presents in several installments the essential affirmations of the Christian faith. Part III is an "Afterward". It is essentially a summary and conclusion drawn from the discussion in the text. Part IV is an addition to the original text. The Guidance, however, points to additional information and study that should be useful to students as well as teachers of the text.

Special thanks have already been expressed to Rev. Patterson of Mount Carmel in reference to the first edition. We have likewise mentioned our gratitude to Dr. Duncan McIntosh as one who helped to bring to the light of day this second edition. It would be remiss not to mention the constant support I received from Ms. Kristy Arnesen of the National Ministries Evangelism Staff of the American Baptist Churches in the USA. It was she who responded to my incessant inquiries as I prepared the text. Then, there is an awareness that it was Mrs. Ruth Fox who blended her knowledge of religion, grammar and word processing to produce a presentable document for publication. Mrs. Fox has become a regular member of my support staff at Eastern Baptist Theological Seminary. I wish to publicly thank her for her efficient and loyal support in the preparation of manuscripts. These and other persons have made this publication possible. I take full responsibility for any shortcomings that may be found. It is my hope that this edition of *Christian Beliefs* will lead many to a saving knowledge of the Christian faith and that it will aid them on their journey to that city which hath foundation, whose Ruler and Maker is God.

Preface to the 2000 Edition

As a result of many requests, this volume is again being made available to the public, especially to church members. It will fulfill an educational purpose for ministers, laypersons and youth.

I am especially grateful for the labors of my youngest daughter, Kristina LaFerne, who through her skills in word processing and editing has prepared this work for release. The printers, Morris Publishing, have also been generous in the role they have played in producing this volume in a prompt and efficient manner.

All members of my family provide a constant source for encouragement as I extend my ministry through publications. My gratitude is hereby expressed to them.

J. Deotis Roberts
Research Professor of Theology
Duke Divinity School
Spring 2000

PART I
FOUNDATIONS

Chapter 1
The Bible as Source Book

"the words that I speak unto you, they are spirit, and they are life" (John 6:63)

Word Study

Bible - English word from the Greek *biblos*, meaning "book".
Gospels - name for the first four books of the New Testament. They are believed to contain the saving core of the Christian message.
Old Testament - refers to the "old covenant" or the first thirty-nine books of the Protestant Bible.
New Testament - refers to the "new covenant" or the last twenty-seven books of the Protestant Bible.
Letters - the several correspondences written from person to person or to congregations during New Testament times.
Word - from the Greek word *logos*, meaning reason, thought, or idea. The Hebrew meaning is more "to speak". The biblical meaning as a whole is in the direction of redemptive thinking and speaking.

The Bible is the most important source of our knowledge of God. We need, therefore, to look at the Bible at once. We must seek to understand how it came to be written and how best to interpret it. The Bible is the key to our knowledge of God and what is required of us.

The Bible as a whole is important, but it is not all on the same level. What Christians find in the New Testament, and especially through the life, ministry, teaching, death and resurrection of Jesus Christ, serves as a standard by which they seek understanding of the entire Bible. Not only what the Old Testament tells us as it points to Jesus but also what has been discovered by Christian experience in the nearly twenty centuries since the earthly life of Jesus help us to understand our Christian faith.

The Bible is a very large work. It contains sixty-six books. Much of the Bible was passed along by word of mouth for a long time before it was written down, and thus it is impossible to know who were the original authors of all the books of the Old Testament. Even in the New Testament, the four Gospels were written from fragments and were not put into their present form until some forty years after the death of Jesus. Paul's letters to the newly formed churches were written earlier than the Gospels. It was the faith of early Christians that prompted the compiling of the rest of the New Testament.

Christian scholars have done much research on various parts of the Bible. The Bible has been examined from the point of view of history. Studies have been made to find out, as far as possible, who wrote each book, when and where it occurred, and the conditions (both religious and social) under which the writing was done.

Other studies are literary in nature. An attempt is made to determine the accuracy of the translations we have on the texts from which they were written. As a result we have a better knowledge of the Bible than was previously possible. We are able to observe the unity of its message in spite of its varied literary forms.

The Bible is now known to have been developed in stages to its present form, and it reflects the attitudes of its authors and the conditions under which they wrote. The Bible is a message *from* God *through* humans. Through its words God speaks, and has been speaking for many centuries, to inspire humans to deeper faith and holy living.

The Bible is the Word of God, regardless of the limitations of the human words through which it comes to us. In spite of its several authors and their social settings, the Bible has a unity in its central message of God's love, mercy, and compassion for people, even in their sinfulness. Though the Bible is not to be taken *literally*, it is to be taken *seriously*. We should read it as we would an important message from a dear friend sent by a middle person. God's Word is spoken through the human words of the writers of the books of the Bible. In our next chapter we will point to an understanding of these divine Words spoken to us today through these very human words.

Bible Reading: John 5:39-47

In this passage Jesus urged his hearers to search the Scriptures. They are said to contain information concerning eternal life. They also testify of him. Later, in verse 46, Jesus indicated that Moses wrote about him. This would seem to imply the continuity of the message of the Old and New Testaments and that all Scripture bears witness to the saving revelation of God through Jesus Christ.

Study Questions

1. Is the entire Bible on the same level?
2. How many books are in the Bible?
3. How was the Bible compiled?
4. Do we know the original authors of the books of the Bible?
5. Which books of the New Testament were written first? The Gospels? The letters of Paul? Explain.

Scripture References for Additional Study

Psalm 19

Describes God's Word in nature and in writing compared to our words about God.

Isaiah 50
Encourages us to listen to God's obedient servant.
II Timothy 4:1-5
Gives Paul's instructions for using God's Word.

PART I
FOUNDATIONS

Chapter 2
The Living Word

"And the Word was made flesh..." (John 1:14)

"the words that I speak unto you, they are spirit,
and they are life" (John 6:63b)

"the worlds were framed by the word of God..." (Hebrews 11:3a)

Word Study

Covenant - an agreement between two parties, i.e., between God and Israel.
Holy Land - the land of Palestine; the birthplace of Judaism as well as Christianity.
Canaan - originally known as the biblical "Promised Land", the destination of the Israelites as they left Egyptian bondage.
Egypt - the land where the Israelites were enslaved in early times.
Abraham - known as the first patriarch or father of the faithful in Israel, i.e., Abraham, Isaac, and Jacob.
Moses - the one who led the Israelites out of Egyptian bondage; Hebrew leader, prophet, and lawgiver.
The living Word - used here in reference to Jesus Christ.
God's Word - Jesus Christ. The words of the Bible bear witness to God's Word as it is revealed in Jesus Christ.

The Bible is a living book. It speaks to you and to me here and now. It is not to be treated as a magical object. It contains messages that come from God to humanity in history. The lives of the characters in the Bible are much like our own. Human nature remains rather constant. Therefore, one is able to identify one's conditions, anxieties, and concerns with one or several persons in the Bible. By reliving their experiences, the words from God to them may become the words of forgiveness, grace, and hope for us in our time and place.

By sitting and standing with the people of the Bible, we get insights into God's dealings with humans and what is required of us. The covenant between God and Israel in the Old Testament is a model for our relationship with God and our concern for others. When Harry Emerson Fosdick visited the Holy Land, he retraced the steps of the Israelites from Egypt to Canaan. He did not take the journey by plane over the desert of Sinai but *through* the desert on foot and on camel's back. The hunger, thirst, and fatigue he experienced helped him share the experiences of the Israelites. He understood much better why a rocky and comparatively unproductive country like Palestine could be for the Israelites a land of promise or "a land flowing with milk and honey".

Many visitors to Palestine have lacked the common sense of Dr. Fosdick. They have expected a perfect physical environment but have not found one. Those who visit the Holy Land with the minds of tourists find it the greatest disappointment of their lives. But, for those who relive the experiences of the People of God in the Old Testament, even the stones have meaning. Indeed, a pilgrimage of Palestine can be a mountain-peak experience of the Christian life if one will retrace the steps of Abraham, Moses, Jesus, or Paul.

We are to understand the Bible as God speaking to us as we *are,* not as we *ought* to be. The Bible gives an accurate account of human life. The people of the Bible are often dreadful sinners in need of salvation. Even the best characters in the Bible reveal many weaknesses under the careful eye of God's judgment. God as Creator, Redeemer, and Judge confronts us where we are-not to condemn, but to save.

The Bible is the living Word of God insofar as it bears witness to God's revealing the divine mind and will to us in Jesus Christ. The supreme norm of the Christian faith is the Word made flesh. God comes to us savingly in Christ. We must never substitute the written words of the Bible for the living Word. The New Testament nowhere applies the Word of God to Scripture. The tendency to identify Scripture with the Word of God came after the New Testament was written. God's Word is God's saving act in Jesus Christ.

God takes the written word up into the living Word-this act is by agency of the Holy Spirit. There is an important relationship between the written and the living Word. There is a union between the Scripture and the living Word in Christ. We must, therefore, use our best knowledge and judgment to interpret Scripture. The Word of God is contained *in* Scripture, and the Scripture is the Word of God insofar as it *bears witness to* the Living Word of God revealed to us in Jesus Christ.

In our next chapter we will provide some further details and guidelines on the study of the Bible. After that we will enter into a study of basic Christian beliefs with the Bible as our main text.

Bible Reading: John 1:1-14

Jesus is described as the Word of God. The Word is the agent of creation as well as the author of salvation. Life, light, and love are marks of the presence and power of the Word. Through faith in God's Word we are saved from sins and become heirs of eternal life. The Word is enfleshed or incarnated in Jesus Christ. Knowledge of God as well as salvation comes through Jesus Christ.

Study Questions

1. Give two reasons why the Bible is a "living book".
2. Does the Bible come to us through humans? Explain.
3. Were people in the biblical world radically different from people today?
4. How may we best enter into the experience of the people of the Old Testament?
5. What is the enduring message of the Bible?

Scripture References for Additional Study

Psalm 78:1-8

The words witness to the acts of God.

Jeremiah 5:1-14

Misuse of the Word of God is breaking the covenant.

Hebrews 1:1-14, 14--2:4

The Word of God came in many ways and continues to be passed on.

PART I
FOUNDATIONS

Chapter 3
The Living Bible: The Old Testament

"The grass withereth, the flower fadeth: but the word of our God shall stand forever" (Isaiah 40:8)

Word Study

logical - from the Greek word *logos*, meaning reason. Thus the sense is reasonable.
chronological - from the Greek word *chronos*, meaning time that is measured, i.e., clock time.
Pentateuch - Genesis to Deuteronomy; the five books of Moses; the books of Law; in Hebrew it is called the Torah, which means teaching or instruction.
Yahweh - for YHWH, the four-lettered Hebrew name of God.
Elohim - another name for God in the Pentateuch.
prophet - one who opens self to God as spokesperson. One who tells God's will as the Spirit gives him or her utterance.
Major/Minor Prophets - the same weight should be given to the message of each prophetic book. Reference should be understood to refer to the size of the book. For example, the twelve minor prophets once formed a single scroll, somewhat equivalent in size to half of Isaiah.
Exile - the period of Jewish captivity in Babylon during the Old Testament period (circa 586 BC and following years).

The Bible is not only a basic source of knowledge for Christian faith but also a profound influence on all Western culture. Biblical themes and quotations appear in masterpieces of literature, art, and music. They are found in historic documents and great political addresses. A moving part of President Kennedy's funeral was composed of readings from the Bible. Many of these Scripture passages had been used by the late president in his many addresses. Our present day morality, at its best, is dependent upon the Bible. Its roots are in the biblical demand for responsibility before God, the concern for one's neighbor, the worth of persons everywhere, and the need of liberty and justice for all.

Since the Bible is a very large book, it is not easy to introduce it adequately. Here we shall give some idea of the variety and range of its literature and the nature of its vital message.

The Old Testament belongs to Jews, Christians, and Muslims. The Jews regard the Old Testament, but not the New Testament, as Scripture or Holy Writ. The Muslims draw upon the entire Bible but regard the Koran as their main scripture. To Christians, the New Testament is more basic because it tells of the life, ministry, and teachings of Jesus. Furthermore, it tells of the redemptive significance of the death and resurrection of Christ and the work of the Holy Spirit. But the Old Testament is also an essential part of the Christian Scriptures because it tells much about God and points towards the coming of Jesus, the Messiah and Savior. The link between the two testaments or covenants of the Bible is that of promise to fulfillment. Hence, the Bible may be said to be a unity-in-diversity. The Christian, upon accepting Jesus Christ as the "author and finisher" of his or her faith, reads the whole Bible with a deeper understanding of the mind and will of God as revealed in Jesus Christ.

The Old Testament contains several books of history. It is a valuable source of Hebrew history. Much of the Old Testament was passed along by word of mouth for a long time before it was written down. Thus, we do not know who all the original authors were or where and when all the books were written. Dedicated Christian and Jewish scholars, who have made a careful study of the history and text of various books of the Bible, have contributed much to a better understanding of Scripture.

The Old Testament is presented in *logical* rather than *chronological* order. What stands first in the Bible was not written first. The earliest writing of history took place about 1000 BC in the stories of Samuel, Saul, and David. David had a court recorder who kept an accurate record of events.

The first five books of the Bible, called the Pentateuch, and most of Joshua and Judges were put into their present form later than the historical books mentioned above. About 850 BC and again about 750 BC, two different strands of the often-recited and well-remembered history of Israel were compiled. When the Temple was being repaired in 621 BC, the Book of Deuteronomy was recovered. The priests, who were held in high regard after the Babylonian exile, compiled the extensive law codes and gave shape to our present Pentateuch beginning with the creation story. The records of the period immediately after the exile have been gathered and presented by Ezra and Nehemiah.

Some scholars attribute the major work on the Pentateuch to Moses. They allow, however, that he compiled Genesis from the oral tradition and other persons after Moses added to the laws and completed his story with the account of his death. Few claim that Moses wrote the entire Pentateuch without reference to earlier stories or without help from a later scribe. To call them the Five Books of Moses simply means that Moses is the principle character in them.

Christian scholars have been most concerned with the major prophets because of their contribution to our understanding of truths that are important to Christian faith and life. There are two prophets known as Isaiah who lived about 150 years apart. The second part of Isaiah is of great value to Christians. It speaks of a coming Redeemer and describes the role of the Suffering Servant. It contributes much to our understanding of the person and saving work of Jesus Christ.

Finally, we observe poetic literature in the Old Testament. There is poetry in the writings of the prophets, but there are other types as well. Since Hebrew poetry is more *thoughtful* than *rhythmical*, the line between prose and poetry is not always clear. The Book of Job is not only poetry but also philosophy. It wrestles with the problem of evil and suffering. The Book of Psalms, a collection of hymns written over many centuries, is greatly loved by both Jews and Christians. Other poetic books are Proverbs, Ecclesiastics and the Song of Solomon.

Two other Old Testament books containing moving stories are Ruth and Jonah. We are now aware of the rich variety of types of literature in the Old Testament. There is a wide range of characters, social settings, and subject matter, and yet throughout the Old Testament, as throughout the whole Bible, God is presented as Creator, Ruler, Judge, and Liberator of all people. The love and mercy of God, even for erring and sinful humankind, is clear. Next we will provide a similar analysis of the New Testament and describe the unity-in-diversity of the entire Bible.

Bible Reading: Isaiah 40:1-8

This passage has been interpreted as one which anticipates the person and work of Christ as Redeemer. It says much about the concern and care God has for humanity. God brings comfort, strength, and pardon to God's people. God reveals and speaks about salvation; God acts and brings forth redemptive change in history. In contrast to flesh, which is like grass that fadeth and withereth, God's Word is everlasting, eternal.

Study Questions

1. What is the historical value of the Old Testament?
2. How did the Old Testament grow into a written book? Describe the history and process of this growth.
3. Give this history of the first five books of the Old Testament. Why do they come first?
4. What books are known as "major" prophets and why?
5. Summarize the value of this study for your understanding of the Old Testament.

Scripture References for Additional Study

Deuteronomy 4:1-24

There is a relation between the character of God and God's Word.

Acts 8:26-35

The Old Testament explains God's redemptive plan.

Hebrews

Why is this called a revision of the Old Testament? How does it reflect a "living book" rather than a "static book"?

PART I
FOUNDATIONS

Chapter 4
The Living Bible: The New Testament

"...my words shall not pass away" (Matthew 24:35)

"...This day is this scripture fulfilled in your ears" (Luke 4:21)

"That which was from the beginning, which we have heard, which we have seen with our eyes, which we have looked upon, and our hands have handled, of the Word of Life" (I John 1:1)

Word Study

apocalyptic - refers to a type of literature and realm of thought (200 B.C.-A.D. 100) that dealt with hidden revelations concerning the end of the present world order. It makes use of "veiled" language and indirect communication. It is often used by the oppressed for exchange of messages in times of persecution (i.e., Daniel and Revelation).
Pharisee - a member of an ancient Jewish sect that accepted the Mosaic Law and the oral traditions associated with it. This party emphasized strict observance of ritual.
Savior - one empowered to forgive sins.
Synoptic Gospels - "similar" Gospels. Reference to Matthew, Mark, and Luke.
Apocalypse of John - the book of Revelation.
holy - set apart for a sacred purpose; a purified or a consecrated object or life.

Christian Beliefs

The New Testament is much shorter than the Old Testament. Its structure is also simpler. Whereas the time span of the Old Testament covers between one and two thousand years, the New Testament reports events that occurred within a little over one hundred years. There are three main types of literature to be found in the New Testament. These are (1) the four Gospels and the book of Acts, in which we have an account of events sprinkled with conversation and sermons; (2) the letters of Paul and others, addressed to the churches; and (3) the book of Revelation, which is a type of literature called apocalyptic-a veiled manner of expression similar to the Book of Daniel in the Old Testament.

The Letters

The letters of Paul were written before the Gospels and Acts. Paul, a Jew of the sect of the Pharisees who was devoted to Jewish law and who persecuted the Christians, became converted on the Damascus Road. He then became a great leader and champion of Christianity. We know Paul as a preacher, evangelist, and church organizer.

As Paul traveled from place to place, he founded new congregations. Then he kept in touch with them, revisiting them sometimes but also writing letters to encourage them. Many of these letters have been saved so that they form the earliest part of the New Testament.

There are nine of these letters that bear the names of churches to which Paul addressed them. These are Romans, First and Second Corinthians, Galatians, Ephesians, Philippians, Colossians, and First and Second Thessalonians. Philemon is a personal letter to a friend. There are three other personal letters-First and Second Timothy and Titus, which bear Paul's name but which may have been written by Christians later since they reflect a later stage in the development of the church.

In addition to these letters of Paul, there are eight more letters in the New Testament that Paul most certainly did not write. These are Hebrews, James, First and Second Peter, First, Second, and Third John, and Jude. Of the twenty-seven books of the New Testament, twenty-one are messages of fellowship to other Christians in particular situations.

The Gospels and Acts

The four Gospels and the book of Acts may be considered together because the author of the Gospel of Luke wrote Acts. Luke-Acts was probably one book at first. The separation was made in order to place the four accounts of Jesus' life and ministry together.

The Gospels deal mainly with the events of Jesus' public ministry, his teaching and healing, and his crucifixion and resurrection. Matthew and Luke give the other information concerning his early life. There is the one incident of his going with his parents to the temple at Jerusalem when he was twelve. We learn no more about him until he began his ministry, when he was baptized by his cousin John the Baptist in the river Jordan at age thirty. This is the sum of what the Gospel writers tell us about the early life of Jesus. Though they say much about his ministry, they devote one-fourth of the entire account to the events of Jesus' last week on earth. His crucifixion and resurrection are most important to the Gospel writers.

Mark, the earliest of the four Gospels, was written no later than AD 70. Mark's account goes directly to the baptism and ministry of Jesus with no reference to his birth and parents. Matthew was written next. In this account the author used Mark's account of the ministry of Jesus and a collection of the sayings of Jesus, now lost except as used by Matthew throughout his book. Luke drew from the same sources as Mark and Matthew but did not stress the same matters. To Mark, Jesus was the miracle-working Messiah; to Matthew, Jesus was the fulfillment of Old Testament prophecy and the Savior promised to Israel. Luke showed the human and compassionate side of Jesus. Luke was more concerned than the others with the universal outreach of the Gospel. Since Luke was a non-Jew and a physician (of the apostle Paul), it is not too difficult to understand his varied interests. In Luke we find some of Jesus' greatest parables, such as the stories of the Good Samaritan and the prodigal son. Luke-Acts has become a primary source for liberation theologies as these emphasize Jesus' concern for setting free the oppressed.

The first three Gospels are more alike than they are different. For this reason they are called the Synoptic Gospels, which means "seeing with one view". The fourth Gospel, John, is believed to have been written toward the end of the first century AD. It reflects more than the others do what the faith of the early church had come to be. All of the Gospels do this to some degree. We do not find in the Gospels a complete biography of Jesus or an exact record of his teaching. Rather we have the portrait of Jesus as the church thought of him. We have an adequate picture for Christians to see in Jesus the revelation of God. We are introduced to the "author and finisher of our faith" (Hebrews 12:2) through the eyes of those who knew, remembered, and loved him.

The book of Acts is the story of the birth of the Christian church. Almost at the beginning is the account of Pentecost, when the Spirit of God, or the Holy Spirit, came upon the new fellowships. Acts gives an account of the preaching and witnessing of the apostles as they struggled against great odds. The conversion and work of Paul are related in Acts, and we are introduced to many problems that had to be met when Gentiles as well as Jews were brought into the Christian church. This book is a vivid account of how Christ's followers put their faith to work.

The Apocalypse of John

This book is also known as Revelation. The word "apocalypse" means vision. This book grew out of the time of severe persecution that Christians had to endure toward the end of the first century. Because it was not possible to speak of the faith openly, its author used veiled language to convey a message of hope and courage to those suffering for their faith. It is a most difficult book to understand. It speaks of hope, of better days to come on earth, and of eternal life in the presence of God.

The Bible as the Living Word of God

From our survey of the Bible we can no longer speak of its message as being spoken directly by God. Some Christians believe that everything in the Bible came directly from God and is without error. This position cannot be defended except by a blind faith. When we study the Bible with our eyes open to truth, we find it to be a very "human" book in its authorship. A careful literary and historical study of the Bible does not take away any meaning from the Bible. We can still believe that it is our main source of knowledge of God and what God requires of us.

The Bible is the Word of God because God speaks through it to us. It is not a mechanical speaking, like a phonograph record, but a *living* medium through which God speaks to us even yet. It is through the Bible, read in faith with an open mind and heart and under the inspiration of the Holy Spirit, that we best learn from God-of what God has done and is doing for humankind. Whereas the written words of the Bible are touched with human frailty, the living Word that used this human instrument is the real divine inspiration of the Bible. The Bible is "holy" because in spite of its imperfections on the human side, the holiness of God still shines through it.

In the Old Testament we see God leading the Hebrew people forward and, through their prophets and seers, instilling a great hope of a coming Messiah who would be their Redeemer and Savior. In the New Testament we see how this hope was fulfilled in the coming of Jesus, who through his teaching and ministry and his death and resurrection, brought into the world from God a new source of light and redemption of life through the gospel, or good news of salvation.

The next important source of Christian theology is "tradition"-the developing thought of the Christian faith through the ages. Thus, we address ourselves to tradition in our next chapter.

Bible Reading: Luke 4:16-21

This passage has been selected as a favorite text for those who view the gospel as good news for the poor and the oppressed. It is a textual foundation for a message of deliverance for those who are poor, brokenhearted, blind, bruised, and imprisoned. While it speaks to the afflictions of personal sin and guilt, the special emphasis of the text implies assurances to victims of social sins as well.

Study Questions

1. What is the period of time covered in the New Testament? Compare this with Old Testament history.
2. What are the three main types of literature found in the New Testament?
3. Which books of the New Testament were written first?
4. What is the relation between Luke and Acts?
5. Summarize the unity of the Bible in its message of redemption and hope.

Scripture References for Additional Study

Isaiah 6:1-11

Why would Jesus have used this passage as his inaugural speech? What meaning is there in it for us?

James 2:8-26

Note how this builds on Leviticus 19:18. Its application is broader than Matthew 5.

PART I
FOUNDATIONS

Chapter 5
The Living Tradition

"That if thou shalt confess with thy mouth the Lord Jesus, and shalt believe in thine heart that God hath raised him from the dead, thou shalt be saved" (Romans 10:9)

"Think not that I am come to destroy the law, or the prophets: I am not come to destroy, but to fulfill" (Matthew 5:17)

Word Study

tradition - beliefs, practices, and standards of conduct from the past.
resurrection - refers to life beyond death, especially Jesus being raised from the dead.
canon - *standard* or *rule* of faith. Refers to those books collected by the church and accepted as authoritative for the Christian faith.
creeds - from Latin *credo*, "I believe". Creeds are usually a collective witness often involving an ecumenical affirmation of basic doctrines of the church. Some creeds belong to particular denominations as well.
dogma - a doctrine or system of doctrines maintained by a religious body as true and necessary for belief and for salvation.
confession - a clear avowal of faith or of sin. It is a firm affirmation as to what one believes or a fervent confession of sin together with a sincere desire to be forgiven.

Introduction: Tradition and Traditionalism

It is important to distinguish between "traditions" and "traditionalism". Tradition has to do with an accumulation of wisdom from your past. It is living, vital, dynamic, and changeable. Traditionalism is static and will not change. Those who live by traditionalism live by a frozen and dead body of dogma (beliefs) wrapped in the past. Tradition, on the other hand, is a proper orientation in the past. It is important to examine the moral and spiritual wisdom of the past in order to find a proper stance for the present and the future. A person without a spiritual history is like someone with *amnesia* or a loss of memory.

Whereas natural science is not to a great extent dependent upon its past, religion is. The same is true of philosophy and morality. Christianity, which combines morality and religion, cannot deny or ignore its past. We need to know our spiritual heritage for the sake of our present and future. What Jesus rejected among the Jewish leaders was traditionalism in the form of legalism. He did not come to "destroy" but to "fulfill" the law and the prophets. The law and the prophets were a part of a live tradition. In the Sermon on the Mount, Jesus frequently moved from the "Ye have heard" to "But I say to you". By translating the past into relevant moral and religious truths, our Lord brought into being a living, vital, saving tradition.

The Meaning of Tradition

The word "tradition" has several meanings. It can be used to mean some historical information that stems from the early church but is independent of Scripture. It can be used to mean a separate source of Christian information and doctrine derived directly from Christ and his apostles-as such it is a supplement to the New Testament. It can mean the doctrine of the church as it has been taught and developed from the earliest time. It can be used for the whole teaching of the church, things taught and the manner of teaching, the development of the teaching, and everything that is handed down from the beginning in Christianity-gospel, doctrine, ethics, order, practice, and custom. It can be applied to the Bible alone, to the church alone, or to the councils alone. But in a general sense there are several "traditions" both in the Bible and the history of the church. But here we are concerned with tradition in its most general, historical, and all-embracing sense as contributing creative, original, and authentic insights to the Christian faith as a supplement for the Bible. Tradition has produced, nurtured, and sustained the Bible, but it also adds the "faith of the church" as a universal fellowship through two thousand years of history. The God who speaks to us in the Bible continues to encounter us through documents, creeds, confessions, councils, and the saintly lives of Christians through the ages.

The Oral Traditions

The Christian tradition was originally passed on by word of mouth-called an oral tradition. Our Lord left no written records behind him after his earthly ministry. The book of Acts is the earliest history of the church. Since this book was written in the latter part of the first century, after Paul wrote his letters, it suggests that no one thought of writing down an account of the works and words of Jesus for several years after the resurrection. The most important reason for this was the conviction that the world was about to end with the Second Coming of Christ. It was believed that a tradition in written form was not needed, for no one can see the value of history when the universe is about to collapse and history itself is near an end. The oral tradition must have been passed from teacher to pupil or from preacher to audience for some time before any of the oral tradition was put into writing. The New Testament is evidence of the transition from an oral to a written tradition.

Even after the New Testament was written, there remained an oral tradition that continued in the early church. Some of this material was later written down in gospels, acts, epistles, and apocalypses (similar to Revelation) that were not included in the New Testament. The oral tradition about Jesus must have continued beyond the first century. Gradually the New Testament, with its select group of books, became the accepted authority within the church. By about AD 170 the New Testament was almost in its present form. It was taken into the "canon" along with the Old Testament. "Canon" means reed, standard or measuring rod. The Bible was thus considered the measure or standard for faith and practice. Up until the books of the New Testament were placed in the canon, the oral and written traditions existed side by side in the church. But the oral tradition faded out as a result of the increasing authority of the written record now known as the New Testament.

Creeds, Confessions and Dogmas

Creeds and confessions are the formal statements of Christian teaching that were drawn up by church councils for the purpose of refuting or rejecting views that were thought to be contrary to Christian teaching or that threatened to undermine the whole Christian religion. Dogmas are the explicit, authoritative, formulated definitions of Christian faith that various churches require their members to accept. Protestants (Baptists are among these) generally have few such dogmas, whereas the Roman Catholics and Orthodox Christians have many. Creeds arose primarily for the purpose of limiting error or false beliefs that would undermine Christianity. They are not summaries of Christian doctrine as a whole. It would be more appropriate to sing the contents of creeds than to recite them. A hymn is viewed not as a complete definition of religious truth but as merely a statement of certain aspects of the Christian faith.

Christian Beliefs

The first recorded use of a creed in public worship in the West was in Rome in AD 900. Creeds are better understood as social rather than individual affirmations of faith. The famous Nicene Creed begins, in Greek, not "I believe" but "We believe". It is the whole Church proclaiming its faith, not a private individual voicing his or her own theological convictions. It is important for the individual to check his or her understanding of the Christian faith against that of the larger fellowship and through the history of the Christian faith. It is important to distinguish a creed from a credo.

We demand that our religious beliefs be accurate, explicit, factual, and logical. Thus, we have taken creeds as a means to this end. The "Baptist Covenant" is a convenient affirmation of faith for Baptists. Our discussion upon this important statement shall come later in the development of this series. Early Christians relied more than we do upon less logical ways of expressing their deepest beliefs and attitudes. They made use of poems, hymns, paintings, and the example of saintly lives to express their deepest beliefs. But there remains an important place for creeds and confessions of faith-a starting point for theological discourse. Theology brings the minds of men and women into the concerns of religion. Religion without theology is like a body without a skeleton. Theology without conviction based upon personal faith and experience is cold and abstract. It cannot lead to a warm and living faith. Religion without thought is flabby, weak, and sentimental. It degenerates into superstition or pleasant daydreams and will possess little if any real or permanent value. Religious experience and theology complement each other as theory and practice do. Whereas experience gives life and vigor to religion, thought gives structure and steadiness to it.

A Living Tradition

Christianity is one of the great historic religions. The true sources of Christian belief are much deeper than creeds, confessions, or dogmas. They are the whole Christian tradition, from the first century to the present, and before that the whole Hebrew-Jewish tradition that was reflected in the Old Testament and taken over by the early Christians in Palestine. This is a living tradition, refreshed, enriched, and translated for us into new dimensions and horizons by Jesus and the apostles. This living tradition has been voiced in many ways-in hymns, prayers, sacred books, stories, works of art, and in formal theological statements that have been issued from time to time.

The Bible and Tradition

One of the tragedies of Protestantism has been its attempt to replace an infallible (without error) church with an infallible book (the Bible). For Protestants (including Baptists), the ultimate source of Christian beliefs is the Bible. The Bible is seen as the divine revelation in regard to what is contained, recorded, and reflected in its pages. We misunderstand the place of the Bible, however, if we believe that we (by reading the Bible for ourselves) can write our own creed, devise our own theological system, organize our own church, and even ordain ourselves as minister. "The priesthood of believers" might be best understood as our being "priest unto each other". The faith of the individual Christian is to be developed in the context of the faith of the Christian church. The place of the church as the fellowship that teaches Christians faith and morals, as the home of the Christian soul, and as the place of divine worship must not be ignored. It is the church that handed the Bible down to us. It collected and safeguarded the sacred books in days of persecution and then preserved, copied, and recopied them. The church has translated, retranslated, and expounded the Scriptures through many centuries and around the globe. It is the church that still teaches the Christian faith with the Bible open.

Henceforth, we must speak of Scripture and tradition as sources for Christian beliefs. It is not the "literal" Bible, torn from the church's hands or lifted out of the living tradition of life and worship, that is the lone source of Christian beliefs. The Bible is the "religion of Protestants" in the sense that it has a supreme place as a religious authority for them. Christians are to listen for the word within the gospel, the living message from God to us, which is still being transmitted to humans through this ancient collection of sacred writings. But we must remember that the faith of Christians is not *only* faith in a living Bible but also faith in a living tradition nurtured in the church as the Christian fellowship from its beginning to the present.

We are now ready to introduce various doctrines in the Christian affirmation of faith. What do we mean when we say, "We believe in God?" Next we will take up the question of God.

Bible Reading: Matthew 5:17-48

Jesus made it clear in this portion of the Sermon on the Mount that tradition was to be taken seriously. But he was not in bondage to it. The past Jewish religious tradition was viewed as foundational to his teachings. His role was to fulfill. He was concerned about the motives and dispositions of the heart and not merely outward ritual and observance. The principles of the disciple's life are dynamic and never static. The law of retaliation (an eye for an eye) is denounced. Not revenge, but love is the motivating force for servants of the kingdom. The goal is a life of perfection in the sense of constant growth toward spiritual and ethical maturity.

Study Questions

1. What is "tradition" and what is "traditionalism"? How do they differ?

2. How is the authority of the Bible to be understood in relation to tradition?
3. Compare oral tradition with the written record. How did the canon develop? Why do you think other writings were left out of the Bible?
4. Why is history so important for Christian faith?
5. What should we mean when we refer to the Bible as the "religion of Protestants"?

Scripture References for Additional Study
Micah 6
Israel lost both its tradition and its meaning.
Judges 2:6-23
Shows what happens when we stop telling the story!

PART II
CHRISTIAN BELIEFS INTERPRETED

Chapter 6
The Existence of God

"In the beginning God..." (Genesis 1:1)

"...he that cometh to God must believe that he is..."
(Hebrew 11:6)

Word Study

theology - from *theos*, meaning god, and "ology", meaning reason or logic. Literally it means reasoning about god.
anthropology - usually used in reference to the Christian understanding of man. To overcome the sexist flavor of the word, we use "humaneotology" or the Christian understanding of what it means to be human.
evil - a reality or force to be reckoned with that explains the opposition to the good. It appears to be more than the absence of the good. It can be discussed in its moral and/or physical dimensions.

There can be no theology without God. The very word "theology" means God-talk or thinking about God. Whatever we may construct without God will not be a theology. We may develop an anthropology or humaneotology (an interpretation of man or humanity), a Jesusology (an understanding of Jesus as a good person), an ethic (a version of man's moral life), or a mixture of all of these, but not a theology.

The Bible begins where theology has its beginning: "In the beginning God..." The Bible does not present arguments for the existence of God because its authors are aware of God's presence, having experienced God through faith. If one believes in God, no proof of God's existence is necessary. If one does not want to believe in God, no proof is possible. The various arguments to prove the existence of God are valuable for the understanding of those who already believe in God or for those who honestly seek belief.

No one can prove God's existence with such compelling logic that even "the fool who has said in his heart there is no God" must believe. But neither can the nonbeliever prove that God does not exist. It is very important for the believer in God to remember that one has just as much rational evidence in favor of belief in God as anyone may present against such belief. For example, if it be said that the one who believes in God cannot explain the existence of evil in a world created and directed by a God of all-goodness and all-power, the non-believer is just as hardpressed to explain the beauty and goodness in the world.

In the seventeenth century Blaise Pascal summed up the problem of the existence of God well when he said: "The God of Abraham, Isaac, and Jacob is not the God of philosophers but of believers." He continues: "It is the heart that *feels* God, not reason." The author of Hebrews is correct: "...he that cometh to God must believe that he is, and that he is a rewarder of them that diligently seek him." We love the Lord with all our *heart* before we love with our entire *mind*. In this manner the faith we have in God seeks *understanding* concerning what it already *believes*.

Bible Reading: Hebrews 11:1-6

This passage begins by defining faith "as the substance of things hoped for" and "the evidence of things not seen." This is very important in affirming belief in the existence of God.

This importance chapter chronicles the story of faith of the people of God, beginning with the Old Testament. This emphasis upon the meaning and importance of faith is a vital clue to any understanding of God. After all attempts to establish grounds for belief in God, we are told that we must "believe that he is." This is the critical affirmation that comes only by faith.

Study Questions

1. Is it possible to construct a theology without God? Why?
2. Where does the Bible begin on the existence of God? Explain.
3. Is it possible to prove that there is a God to one who does not want to believe? Why?
4. Is it possible to prove that God does not exist? Explain.
5. Is it important to give some thought to why one believes in God? Why?

Scripture References for Additional Study

Isaiah 44:1-22

A contrast between the God of Israel and idols.

Psalm 14; Romans 1:19-32

An Old and New Testament description of the believer and unbeliever. Why would it be true to say what we do, more than what we say, expresses our true belief about God?

PART II
CHRISTIAN BELIEFS INTERPRETED

Chapter 7
God as Personal Spirit

"God is a Spirit..." (John 4:24)

Word Study

spirit - the nonmaterial in the world or beyond. The soul (not the fleshly body) of the human being.
space/time - that which refers to the measurement of human-historical experience. Space is the unlimited expanse in which all material objects are contained. Time implies duration of existence in terms of past, present, and future.
providence - refers to the unfolding of the divine purpose in nature and history.
purpose - an idea, ideal or goal kept before one as an end of effort or action. A design or aim to be effected or attained.
personality - distinctive qualities of a person or personal nature, i.e., mind, will, and emotions.
value - worth of a thing, its intrinsic quality or merit. Can also refer to ideals or principles.
union - one person or thing merges or coalesces into another and assumes its identity. In the case of God and humans, the human merges into God.
communion -one person or thing enters into close association, relation, or fellowship with another without losing identity. In the case of God and humans, the human enters into a close relationship with God without losing human nature.
blessedness - a state of being consecrated: enjoying an exalted quality of life.

happiness - the experience of pleasure or joy.

God is a personal spirit. Spirit has a purpose-it is capable of moral ends. The Christian faith affirms the spirituality of God. Space or time does not limit God as a spirit. God is timeless (God always has been and always will be) and spaceless (God is everywhere at the same time). But God is at work in time (history) and human experience. This is the basis of the belief in God's presence and purpose (providence). Likewise there is no place where God is not. God as spirit is everywhere without being everything. God sees all you do and hears all you say.

Spirit is best understood as being aware of value. God is a conscious mind who is the very embodiment of love and goodness: God is love. God is purposeful mind. God as spirit reveals himself as personal in his approach to the human soul. God does not treat us as *things* but as *persons*, not as *objects* but as *subjects* (selves). Only personality can be sensitive to moral value. God reveals himself to us as *personal love* calling for the *response* in us to accept this love with gratitude of faith and life. A human being is limited and imperfect in personality while God as spirit, as ultimate goodness and love, is limitless and perfect in personal life. Just as we, as personal centers of consciousness, possess the ability to feel, think, and will, God even more so, and in a perfect sense, possesses and exercises mind, passion, and will in a manner consistent with God's moral perfection.

The true end of human life is an "I-Thou" relationship with God. The goal of human life is not *union* but *communion* with God. We do not lose our identity or selfhood in this relationship. The will and purpose of human life should be in tune with God's will. Augustine was right as he confessed: "Thou has made us for Thyself, O God, and our hearts are restless until they find rest in Thee." The goal of human life, then, is to love God and enjoy him forever. This is blessedness that is not the same thing as happiness. In this fellowship with God our own personal life is taken up into the personal life of God and is transformed into God's likeness. In the experience of this higher happiness, one knows a "peace that passes all understanding". Scripture summed up the matter in this way: "Beloved...it doth not yet appear what we shall be: but we know that...we shall be like him; for we shall see him as he is" (I John 3:2).

Bible Reading: John 4:19-24

Jesus encountered a woman who worshipped the spirits of nature. She seemed to associate the presence of the divine with a mountain. Spirits were, therefore, resident in a particular sacred space.

Jesus made it clear that God is a universal spirit whose presence is not confined to a particular space or time. God's presence is everywhere at all times. The focus of approaching God is upon the way one worships God-"in spirit and in truth."

Study Questions

1. Why do we say that God is a personal spirit?
2. What is the importance of the timelessness and spacelessness of God?
3. In what ways are spirit and moral purpose related?
4. How does God make himself known to us?
5. What is the nature of our relationship with God?

Scripture References for Additional Study

Genesis 3:8-24; Job 38

Two different pictures of God: a close companion and an overpowering creator.

Romans 8:1-27

The work of the Spirit of God in our redemption and sanctification.

PART II
CHRISTIAN BELIEFS INTERPRETED

Chapter 8
The Holiness of God

"...God that is holy shall be sanctified in righteousness"
(Isaiah 5:16)

"The Lord is...holy in all his works" (Psalm 145:17)

Word Study

holy - to set apart for a sacred purpose. It implies moral cleanliness, purity from a moral and spiritual point of view.
perfection - a process of maturing toward an ethical ideal. It is a dynamic concept rather than a static, finished state.
rectitude - implies integrity and trustworthiness of character.
profane - secular, earthy, the opposite of sacred or holy.
sanctification - growth in likeness to God's holiness; the process of salvation.

God is Holy. The Hebrew word *Kadosh* had no particular ethical (moral) meaning until it was used by the Old Testament prophets. Isaiah said: "God the Holy One is sanctified in righteousness." Likewise the term most frequently used in the New Testament to signify that which is holy, *haglos* from the Greek, received its distinct meaning from the Christian faith. By rooting "holiness" in the very nature of God, holiness itself was lifted to a higher level. At the same time morality or righteousness was elevated to its highest level.

Holiness in God is transfigured righteousness. God's holiness becomes the supreme example of this crowning ethical virtue. Holiness is the sum of God's goodness, the fullness of God's moral perfection. It implies stainless purity as well as perfect manifestation of the moral ideal. It includes righteousness, justice, truth, and even love itself, since all of these belong to the moral ideal. Holiness is usually associated with (but does not substitute for) rectitude of will rather than with the warmth of affection that is usually associated with divine love.

Again, *Kadosh* means to separate. In a religious sense the word implies that which by association with God has been cut off from profane use. God is holy (Psalm 99:9), or God's name is holy (Psalm 99:3, 111:9). If anything else is holy, it is due to its nearness or contact with God, the Holy One. Things are not by nature holy; rather God's use of them make them holy. In the call of Moses the ground was said to be holy (Exodus 3:5). But this holiness was acquired because God was present and used the ground as sacred space. In like manner the temple was holy for Isaiah because God's presence filled it. God, then, is the author of holiness and for this reason holiness is both personal and moral.

The Christian is aware that perfect holiness is found in God alone. The experience by which one becomes like God is called sanctification. It is the process of becoming holy. To sanctify is to "holify". Christians are persons who are consecrated or set apart by God. But the experience of God's holiness prepares them to be a more effective "leaven" among humans.

Bible Reading: Isaiah 6:1-13

The vision of God is described in terms of God's holiness: "Holy, holy, holy, is the LORD of hosts..." (6:3). The vision is threefold. God's holiness casts in clear relief the profaneness of everything else. The personal and collective sins of humans are revealed for what they are in the presence of the divine cleanliness and purity. The prophet is fully surrounded and engulfed by the presence of the divine holiness of God. He is overawed by the angelic praise to God's holiness. He sees God, himself, and others in the vision. His call to servanthood is to be measured by the profundity of this vision.

Study Questions

1. How was the meaning of the word "holy" changed in the Old Testament?
2. In what way is holiness rooted in the very nature of God?
3. Is there an important relation between holiness and the other attributes of God, i.e., justice, righteousness, and love?
4. How does a person or place become holy? Explain.
5. Explain "sanctify" in relation to God's holiness as an experience of the Christian life.

Scripture References for Additional Study
Leviticus 19 and 20

These chapters build human laws on the holiness of God. What is the meaning of Matthew 5:48 in light of its context in chapters 5 to 7? In John 17 Jesus addresses God as Holy Father. In Acts 3:12-14 Peter called Jesus the Holy One. In light of John 17, why is this appropriate for Jesus?

PART II
CHRISTIAN BELIEFS INTERPRETED

Chapter 9
The Righteousness of God

"...What doth the LORD require of thee, but to do justly, and to love mercy, and to walk humbly with thy God?" (Micah 6:8)

"For they being ignorant of God's righteousness, and going about to establish their own righteousness, have not submitted themselves unto the righteousness of God" (Romans 10:3)

Word Study

righteousness - morally correct or justifiable; upright. Also equitable, just, or virtuous.
justification - to be made righteous in a theological sense. To be forgiven of sins and made right with God.
soteriological - refers to the experience of salvation-that process of being reborn spiritually through the saving work of Christ.

Righteousness in the Old Testament included both justice and mercy. The moral meaning is uprightness; the religious meaning is benevolence and salvation. In the New Testament the Greek word for "righteousness" is *dikaiosune*. It means to justify or to make righteous and has both moral and religious importance.

In the Bible, God is the standard of righteousness rather than the community. That is to say, the biblical understanding of righteousness is theocentric (God-centered) rather than anthropocentric (human-centered). Righteousness, as holiness, is first a quality in God before it becomes a norm for us. God's righteousness is closely associated with God's holiness and uprightness. God is trustworthy. He does not make unfair demands and is just in all his dealings. He requires righteous conduct of his people and will judge them by law. In the light of God's righteousness, human morality is called to its highest and best.

We have looked at God's righteousness as a quality of his life and a norm for human conduct. But God's righteousness is also his activity. God brings certain things to pass by the doing of righteousness. He established righteousness in the world. The great prophets of the Old Testament developed the notion that God would vindicate his people and establish righteousness for them. To the ethical meaning is added a soteriological (redemptive) meaning-God delivers and *saves* his people.

Then, God's righteousness is the state of things that result from his activity. God accomplishes his purpose. This understanding of God in righteousness is bound up with the doctrine of last things or the future life.

Paul viewed the gospel as a revelation of the righteousness of God. God's sending his Son into the world is bound up with God's righteousness. God acts to *save* his people. The coming of Christ does not lessen ethical requirements; it sharpens them, as the Sermon on the Mount indicates. Humanity is sinful and cannot fulfill God's demands alone. The achievement of God's righteousness is possible only through God's help-that is, his grace. God offers his righteousness to us in the person of Jesus Christ. Those who respond in faith to Jesus Christ are accounted righteous.

Righteousness is a quality in God; it is what is required of us in conformity to his holiness. It is that which he bestows through faith in Christ and the result of this activity, the life in Christ which works out this righteousness in love to neighbor.

Bible Reading: Romans 10:1-13

This passage in Paul's letter to the church at Rome is strong in its message of salvation. But it has a lot to say about the righteousness of God and how God's righteousness is essential to his nature. The apostle was preoccupied with the proper knowledge of this attribute of God. He pointed to how Christ is the sure indicator of this knowledge. Moses taught the righteousness of God in the law. Christ, however, is the end of the law. Through Christ the knowledge of God's righteousness comes by faith. God is the righteous One. Through Christ we know of the righteousness of God. It is efficacious to our own salvation-we are made righteous, justified.

Study Questions

1. What does "righteousness" mean in the Bible? In the Old Testament? In the New Testament?
2. In what sense is God the standard of righteousness?
3. Discuss righteousness as viewed by the great prophets, by Jesus, by Paul.
4. In what sense is righteousness a quality? An activity? A state?
5. What is the importance of the coming of Jesus Christ for our understanding of righteousness?

Scripture References for Additional Study

Job was a righteous man (Job 1:1, 22) even though his friends denied it (4:17, 15:14). Job never recanted (27:6) and was ultimately honored by God (Chapter 42). The two questions for Job are:
1) How can I be declared right before God? (9:1-12)
2) How can I argue with God about my righteousness? (9:13-35)
Despite his righteousness (10:15) he is despondent because he can't understand God (10:1-22).

Acts 10:34-43; Revelation 15:3-4; 16:5-7; 19:1-2, 5-8
These passages describe God's righteous judgments.

PART II
CHRISTIAN BELIEFS INTERPRETED

Chapter 10
The Love of God

"...God is love" (1 John 4:8)

"...the God of love...shall be with you" (2 Corinthians 13:11)

Word Study

love - the Hebrew word *chesed* is translated as "covenant love", "loving kindness" or "steadfast love". The Greek words are *eros*; selfish or erotic love; *philia*, brotherly love or a reciprocal love between two persons; and *agape*, an altruistic or unselfish love. Theologically, God is said to be true *agape*.

Love sums up as no other word does the divine life of God. It gathers up the meaning of the righteousness and mercy of God in the Old Testament. About as close as the Old Testament gets to the "love of God" is in its reference to "loving kindness" or "steadfast love", which is likewise called "covenant love". God enters into a covenant with Israel based upon his love. God is faithful or steadfast in keeping his promise, but Israel is often faithless and wayward in respect to God's love. In Hosea and Isaiah 4-66, great emphasis is placed upon God's love.

The love of God is mentioned only once in the first three Gospels (Luke 11:42). But in the Gospel of John and the Letters of John, love is a constant theme in reference to God's nature and his saving activity. Paul wrote a famous "love" poem (1 Corinthians 13) and used love as a dominant theme. This love is shed abroad in our hearts daily (Romans 5:5) by the Holy Spirit who is given to us. John summed up the matter in his first letter when he wrote: "...God is love" (1 John 4:8).

Love in God makes his concern for us very personal. The love of God calls forth a response in us. According to Jesus, love of God and neighbor sum up all the law and the gospel. The love of God is manifest in the self-giving and self-sacrificing action for us humans, of which the cross is the chief symbol. The love of God is made known in the life, death, and resurrection of Jesus Christ. It is the whole content, sum, and substance of the gospel. In love were we created; by love were we redeemed; through love we were sanctified. God is love; love is God.

Bible Reading: 1 John 4:7-16

We demonstrate that we know God through expressing our love to one another. This is clearly not selfish or erotic love. It is grounded in the way God has revealed his love toward us in Christ. God loves us through Christ neither because we first loved God nor because we deserve God's love. The love of God transcends mundane considerations. Our responsibility as Christians is to love in the same way that God has expressed love redemptively to us in Jesus Christ. The confession of faith in Christ includes a commitment to love others as God in Christ has loved us. God is love. To dwell in love is to live in God.

Study Questions

1. What is the importance of the love of God in the Old Testament?
2. What Old Testament books place the greatest stress on the love of God?
3. What writers in the New Testament say most about the love of God?
4. How do we know that God loves us? How may we best respond to God's love?
5. What is the supreme revelation of the love of God?

Scripture References for Additional Study

Psalm 103; Isaiah 43:1-7

The many ways God's love is revealed to us.

John 13:1

The "threshold to the Upper Room" and the passage to His passion.

PART II
CHRISTIAN BELIEFS INTERPRETED

Chapter 11
The Tri-Unity of God

"Go ye therefore, and teach all nations, baptizing them in the name of the Father, and of the Son, and of the Holy Ghost" (Matthew 28:19).

"The grace of the Lord Jesus Christ, and the love of God, and the communion of the Holy Ghost, be with you all" (2 Corinthians 13:14).

Word Study

trinity - refers to the three-in-oneness of God or the threefold manner in which God reveals his mind, will, and purpose to us.
revelation - points to the divine unveiling or self-disclosure.
ousia - means essence or essential reality. It is what something really is at its core of being.
hypostasis - refers to manifestation or how something or someone reveals itself or oneself to outside persons or things. It points to external relations or effects.
personae - originally, party or parties in a law court. Also "dramatic personae," i.e., an actor or actress playing more than one role. It implies the ways in which a thing or person expresses its essence or nature.
personality - a term with a basic psychological meaning, i.e., St. Augustine's memory, understanding, and will. Modern description of the self in terms of mind, will, and emotion. Reference is to one entity that has multiple modes of self-expression.

The doctrine of the trinity explains the divine as Father, Son, and Holy Spirit. It tells us something about the internal life of God and something about his external relations with humanity and the world. The trinity deals with the tri-unity or three-in-oneness of God. The concern of the doctrine is not with numbers (how *three* can be *one*) but with the three *ways* or manners through which the one God *relates* and makes himself *known* to us.

In other words, we are describing through this doctrine the experience of the first Christians with God. We must understand the *nature* and *manner* of God's revelation to us in order that we may find meaning from the doctrine of the trinity. Revelation is divine *unveiling*, the way God makes himself known to us. According to the Christian faith, God reveals himself to us as Lord in a threefold manner as Father, Son, and Spirit.

The Bible does not provide us with a clearly stated doctrine of the trinity, but the *root* of the belief is based upon the witness of Scripture. The Scripture relates how believers experienced God's *presence* and *power* in a threefold manner. The trinity tells both about the threesomeness of God's inner life and the three basic manifestations of the unfolding of God's mind and will to us.

The need for a statement of belief in the trinity arose when the Christian faith confronted Greek culture. The Greek words *ousia* and *hypostasis* were used in the ancient creeds to express the doctrine of the trinity. *Ousia* means essence, nature or content. *Hypostasis* refers to the way something appears or *manifests* itself to us. God, according to the Christian faith, is one, but he appears to us in a threefold manner (in a *threeness*) as Father, Son, and Spirit. It was usual for one Greek actor to play a number of roles in a single play by changing costumes-one *ousia* in several manifestations (*hypostasis*). A similar meaning derives from the Latin root for the word "person". The word "persons" as used by the church in reference to the Godhead did not mean personality in the modern sense. The reference is clearly to three aspects of what we now refer to as one personality. Against this background, "God in three *persons*, blessed Trinity" can be meaningful.

We may illustrate the internal life of God by comparing our own personal life with the divine life. As persons we are able to *think, feel,* and *choose* or *will*. But it is only when our life is united around a oneness (a single goal or purpose) that our *thinking, feeling*, and *willing* are healthy or whole. Life is whole when we express the three-in-oneness (the tri-unity) of our personal life. St. Augustine used the figures of memory, understanding, and will. In like manner, the Godhead as Father, Son, and Spirit expresses the "Godness" of God-his goodness, holiness, and love.

The trinity is about the saving experience in which God reveals himself as Lord. God creates as Father. God redeems a Son. God sanctifies as Spirit. These are his ways of being God and saving us. In this experience we encounter the three-in-oneness of God, a unity-in-trinity, a trinity-in-unity.

Bible Reading: John 16:7-15

The Bible is satiated with Trinitarian insights, but it does not present any Trinitarian dogma. The passage selected here is one indication. Jesus who had come from God, the Father, spoke of the coming of the Spirit to continue God's saving work. Jesus spoke of the Spirit as one who will bring truth, comfort, and righteousness. The Spirit will also guide the believer as he or she teaches. As Jesus completed his earthly mission, he pointed to the Spirit as the one who will continue to represent the work of the Father and the Son in the Christian life and experience. The Bible, and here Jesus, present the trinity of religious experience. The one God continually carries on a saving work among humans in all his manifestations.

Study Questions

1. What is the basic concern of the doctrine of the trinity?
2. How important is the doctrine of revelation to the trinity? Explain.
3. Is the trinity clearly and fully developed in the Bible?
4. How did the doctrine of the trinity develop and why?
5. What are some meaningful illustrations of the trinity? Explain.

Scripture References for Additional Study

Isaiah 40:1-18

The incomparable nature of God: word, act, power!

Ezekiel 37:1-14

God's re-creative breath.

Philippians 2:1-11

God's step from glory to humiliation.

PART II
CHRISTIAN BELIEFS INTERPRETED

Chapter 12
What Does It Mean to Be Human?

"...God created man in his own image, in the image of God created he him; male and female created he them" (Genesis 1:27).

*"What is man that thou art mindful of him,
and the son of man that thou dost care for him?
Yet thou hast made him little less than God,
and dost crown him with glory and honor."
(Psalm 8:4-5)*

Word Study

human - the highest form of life we know. A form of life that is capable of physical, intellectual, and spiritual expression. A form of life that is conscious of and free to make moral choices. Refers to both male and female.
Imago Dei - "image of God." While the Genesis account(s) may use the terms "image" and "likeness", the meaning is one relation between man and God. So far as we know, humans are potentially the most "god-like" creatures. We are also potentially the most demonlike creatures. Apparently one is essential to the other.
creation - that which has originated or been brought into existence by some agent-human or divine.
nature - the essential character of a person or thing.

These words are especially important to remember today when human life seems so cheap and is snuffed out with such indifference. The psalmist speaks of the divine intention for human life. God has exalted us, but we have debased our own nature.

There are many ways to describe human beings. We may be explained in terms of body, mental life, or spiritual life. The Christian understanding of humanity is summed up in the term "image of God," the *Imago Dei*. Human life is precious because we are made in a unique sense "like God" (Genesis 1:26ff, 9:6). What is humanity? Are we a reflection of God's glory? Does the term refer to the state of humans as we now are? Does it refer to us as we *ought to be* or *will be* when restored from our fallen state in sin to God's favor? Christians give a great deal of meaning to the term "image of God." Perhaps the psalmist is correct-God has made us a "little less than God."

A human being is said to be a child of God or a son of God in the New Testament. Whereas the Old Testament speaks of our dignity as we were *created*, the New Testament speaks of our nature as we are *re-created* or redeemed from sin. Our sin has separated us from God, but in and through the saving work of Christ, we have opened to us the possibility of reclaiming our true nature. Luke sums this up in chapter 15 where he tells the story of the prodigal son. Humans, like this wayward son, have been created in the likeness of God but have rejected their heavenly Father's love. We are estranged from that love. But God loves us even as the father loved his lost son in the far country. Recently I saw a mother embrace a son who had been thousands of miles away for many years. As I observed the joyful tears that filled the mother's eyes, I could only say, "God loves like that." Love unites God and humanity. God and humans belong together. We find fulfillment only when we return to our heavenly Father who embraces us in love.

Humans are creatures. We are mortal. But God has given us an exalted place among creatures. Humans live on two levels- as children of nature and as children of God. We must affirm the goodness of our bodily life, for creation itself comes from the hand of a good God. But physical satisfaction is not the true end of life. Our loving relation with God is our true and final end. Thus, we have been given by the "Maker of heaven and earth" the ability to transcend the earthbound aspects of our nature. This transcending takes place in our best moments. To the Christian the "Author of Nature is the Giver of Grace." We were made for God, and our souls are fulfilled only in communion with God, who is the author of our lives and the parent of our spirits.

Bible Reading: 1 Corinthians 15:21-22, 45

These verses are set in the fifteenth chapter of First Corinthians, a rich passage of Pauline theology. Much of Paul's contribution to our understanding of the saving work of Christ and the future life is stated boldly and profoundly here. The passage also states the relationship between the creation of humans by God and the restoration of a redemptive relation between humans and God after the fall. Thus we encounter the created/fallen humanity. Adam and Eve represent the trans-gressed and sinful human, while Christ represents reconciled humanity. It is through the saving work of Christ, who intercedes before God on our behalf, that we as humans are redeemed.

Study Questions

1. What are some reasons why we should consider the Christian understanding of humanity today?
2. What is the importance of the "image of God" figure for Christians?
3. What is meant by the term "child of God" in the New Testament?

4. How does Luke 15 cast light upon the conditions of humanity and God's love for us?
5. We live in two worlds. Explain. What does this imply for a Christian view of humanity?

Scripture References for Additional Study
Genesis 2:4b-25
Our purpose.
Psalm 39
Our fragility.
Romans 7:7-25
Our struggle.
Revelation 21:1-8
Our hope.

PART II
CHRISTIAN BELIEFS INTERPRETED

Chapter 13
Sin as a Universal Reality

"For all have sinned, and come short of the glory of God" *(Romans 3:23).*

"...Father, I have sinned against heaven, and before thee" *(Luke 15:18; cf. v. 21).*

Word Study

moral - having to do with ethical judgment, decision, or behavior. Choosing between good and evil, right and wrong.
evil - morally bad, wicked. That which causes injury or undesirable results, such as harm, misfortune, distress, or disaster. Evil is a real existence and presence that opposes that which is good and right.
sin - is moral evil. It results from separation from God as the true end of human life. It is willful disobedience to God's requirements. It involves a choice of evil ends over good ends, and it results in a series of broken relationships-with God, self, and other persons.

We have indicated before that we are not as we ought to be. Human nature as we know it is a good thing that has been spoiled. Sin has to do with moral wrongs, but most of all it has to do with a broken relation with God. Wrong conduct is a signal that something has gone wrong within. Sins of flesh indicate sins of the spirit.

God created humans as part of a good creation. The Creator gave human beings an exalted place within that creation. We were endowed with the ability to think and to exercise freedom of choice. We were given "the knowledge of good and evil." Humans have perverted all these gifts. We have said yes to self and no to God. In doing this we have cut ourselves off from the source of our life. We have made ourselves miserable and unhappy. "All have sinned."

What does it mean to say, "All have sinned"? Does it mean that parents pass their sins on to their children at birth? Does it mean that sin is universal (is found among all people in all lands) whatever the explanation? It is a fact that sin appears very early in the life of a child and that wherever we travel in the world, that sin is present. How do we explain these facts?

Human freedom is real. We make real choices, but when we do, we are accountable. In view of this, we must understand sin in a way that will support the Christian view of humanity as well as the Christian understanding of God. If sin is inherited, the infant is not free *not* to sin, and the choice of sinning or not sinning is not open to us. Free will and personal guilt are related as are freedom and moral responsibility. To bear the weight of guilt and responsibility, one must be free to choose between good and evil, right and wrong, truth and error.

Then let us assume that one is *really free*-that one does make choices and that, like Adam and Eve, one can say yes or no to God's commands. Yet it is a fact that human society, beginning with family ties, is so filled with sin and evil that from birth the child's future is weighed in a sinful direction. As a little boy put it, "Sinning is like going downhill." This would explain why sin is everywhere among all peoples and why it appears so early in life. This view has the advantage, however, of allowing for personal freedom. This alone explains how a person who comes from the worst type of family or social situation can become a moral and spiritual giant, not *in spite of* the environment, but *because of* it. We need a doctrine of sin that explains not only the *worst* people we know but also the *best*. Even God's grace builds on human dignity and freedom and does not demolish it.

We are sinners by choice. Our nature is a good thing spoiled. We are Adams of our own souls. In the presence of freedom and "the knowledge of good and evil," we have deliberately chosen evil. We have chosen the sinful way even though a better way is both *known* and *possible*. Both knowledge and freedom are available to us to do better, but we choose to do *worse*. Each one is the Adam of his or her own soul. Sin, then, is willful disobedience. Who then would dare question Paul's judgment? Indeed, "All have sinned."

Bible Reading: Romans 3:1-31

This is an appropriate chapter to illustrate the universality of sin. It is a chapter concerned with sin and salvation for all humans, Gentiles as well as Jews. God is the judge of the world (v.6). Jews and Gentiles are all under sin (v.9). None are righteous (v.10). According to the law, all are guilty before God (v.19). The law makes us knowledgeable of sin and of the difference between good and evil. But the knowledge of the righteousness of God through faith in Jesus Christ provides a more profound awareness of sin as a universal reality (vv.21-23). This greater knowledge is accompanied by an assurance that redemption is available also in Jesus Christ.

Study Questions

1. What do we mean when we say, "Human nature is a good thing spoiled"?
2. Describe humans as God intended them to be. What has happened to human beings?
3. What definition of sin is suitable for the Christian understanding of humanity? Explain.

4. Is sin inherited? Give pros and cons. What is your answer? Why?
5. How do we explain the universality of sin and yet retain the freedom and dignity of each person?

Scripture References for Additional Study
Genesis 3:1-21
The root of sin.
Psalm 51
The cure for sin.
Luke 15:11-32
The prevalence of sin.

PART II
CHRISTIAN BELIEFS INTERPRETED

Chapter 14
What Will You Do with Jesus?

"And she shall bring forth a son, and thou shalt call his name JESUS: for he shall save his people from their sins" (Matthew 1:21).

Word Study

Jesus - refers to one who saves from sin.
disciple - one who follows a leader.
publican - tax collector (for the Romans).
messiah - expected deliverer of people.
priest - a religious functionary whose main role is to comfort those in distress.
authority - the power to judge, act, or command.

Wherever there are humans, there is sin. And where there is sin, there is a need for a savior. The question "What will you do with Jesus?" has been constant through the centuries. It is both individual and social. What will *you* do *with* Jesus? Jesus means savior and thus our relationship with him has to do with our salvation. Salvation implies sin, from which we are to be delivered by his saving power. It follows that Jesus is important to the Christian life.

The word "Christian" means to be Christlike or to follow Jesus as his disciple. Our purpose here is to examine the person of the one who came to us as Savior. His example serves as an inspiration to us; it calls forth from us the highest and the best. His life places a crown above our heads that we must stand on tiptoe to wear. Jesus lived as a man in the midst of humanity. He was born in a barn. He identified with the downtrodden--publicans and sinners. Common people were at ease in his presence and hung on his words with eagerness. He was sometimes hungry and thirsty, tired and weary. He was a carpenter's son. He was from Nazareth, an obscure village, which could claim no great personalities. Apparently only thieves and thugs had come from this place. Hence the question, "Can anything good come out of Nazareth?"

Even during his life, Jesus was not easy to identify. The question was raised, "Is not this the son of Joseph?" To various people he was different things. To the religious establishment (the Scribes and Pharisees) Jesus was a troublemaker, an impostor, a false messiah, a revolutionary, an outcast, and a traitor to his people and their religion. But to others Jesus was a friend, a brother, a healer, a prophet, a priest and king. What will you do with Jesus?

Some have questioned the existence of the authority of Jesus, even in recent times. This is not true of those who know him as the one who has saved them from their sins. When Jesus first came to dwell among humans, he found a "no vacancy" sign at the inn. Jesus came to his own, which is to the Jews, but they rejected him. Those who received Him, however, became children of God. Light, truth, and life came into the world with him. Malcolm X, in telling us the story of his life, says that when he learned to read in prison, he became really free. This freedom is but naught when compared with the freedom that Jesus brings to lives enslaved by sin. "If the Son makes you free, you will be free indeed" (John 8:36, RSV). You will be *really free*. "...you shall call him name Jesus for he will save his people from his sins" (Matthew 1:21, RSV).

What will you do with Jesus?

Bible Reading: John 4:4-29

The woman of Samaria found the answer to the question raised in this chapter. She belonged to a group of people for whom the Jews had little respect. Jesus taught the woman the meaning of the abundant life. The Samaritan woman was converted and became a witness to the saving experience she had with Jesus. She was convinced that Jesus was the Christ, the expected deliverer from sin. Even his disciples were surprised that Jesus would give so much attention to a person whom they considered to be an outcast, a nobody. But this is an illustration of the concern Jesus has for sinful and lost souls. He is Savior to the least of these "his little ones". Thus the woman's conclusion was that Jesus was Savior.

Study Questions

1. What does the word "Jesus" mean?
2. Why is the example of Jesus so important to the Christian?
3. In what way does Jesus reach down to the humblest and even meanest levels of human life?
4. Why is it hard to identify Jesus?
5. What benefits come to those who accept Jesus as their Savior?

Scripture References for Additional Study

Psalm 98

A song to the Savior.

Isaiah 60:1-12

The power of the Savior.

Luke 2:8-38

The announcement of the Savior.

PART II
CHRISTIAN BELIEFS INTERPRETED

Chapter 15
"What Think Ye of Christ?"

"Thou art the Christ, the Son of the living God" (Matthew 16:16).

"And we believe and are sure that thou art that Christ, the Son of the living God" (John 6:69).

Word Study

Muslims - those who submit to the will of Allah (God). Followers of the Prophet Mohammed.
Lord - a person who has dominion over others. Bible reference is to YHWH as well as to Jesus Christ.
liberator - a title ascribed to Jesus Christ by liberation theologians. Jesus Christ is said to set us free from all forms of oppression, whether personal, social, or institutional.
Christ - from the Greek *christos* meaning anointed. Thus Christ is said to be the Anointed One.
apostle - one who is sent. Note the distinction from disciple, one who follows.
cosmic - the universe (natural order or creation) as an orderly system. From the Greek *kosmos*, meaning order, world, universe.

The Jesus of history is the Christ of faith. When the question was asked, "What think ye of Christ?" the early Christians replied "He is the Son of God."

In our last lesson, we were more concerned with Jesus the person. It is important for us to know that Jesus shared our humanity--that he was born, that he was hungry and thirsty, that he was sometimes tired and weary, and that he suffered and died. These are human experiences. Jesus was also "tempted like as we are." (Hebrews 4:15). But he did not sin. Jesus was truly human. As the creeds put it, "He was very man." If Jesus, however, were *only* a human being, he could be a worthy *example* but not the Savior of sins. Humans, as sinners, need a savior. This is the reason it is so important for Christians to know that Jesus is the Christ.

The Jews and Muslims accept Jesus as a great prophet. The Jews still look for a savior. The Muslims have a prophet (Mohammed) but no savior. Christians, on the other hand, have accepted Jesus as their Savior, beginning with the disciples and apostles. In the earliest confessions of the Christian faith, Jesus is called "Lord." This lordship of Christ has redemptive importance for believers. Christ is Lord of life and Lord *over* death. Christ is also Liberator of the oppressed and Reconciler of the estranged. His suffering on the cross is understood as being not for himself, the sinless One, but for us, the sinful. His being raised from the dead is viewed as the means by which sinful humans, enslaved by sin to the point of death, might henceforth be raised to "newness of life."

The assertion that Jesus is the Christ (the Messiah) has yet another important meaning. It implies that Jesus is *divine*. Not only is he truly human, he is likewise *very* God "God...was in Christ, reconciling the world unto himself..." (2 Corinthians 5:19). It is important to know that the one who helps us to overcome our sins and weaknesses is not limited by our sinful and finite conditions. Jesus, as the Christ, was sinless as he passed our "human way," but is now raised to power and glory. He can be our Lord, or Savior, and make us "heirs of the kingdom." A human being cannot do this. Even the best humans are fallen and unable to save themselves. Surely they cannot save us. But the one who is *very* man and *very* God, the God-man, the one who is both *human* and *divine*, is able to redeem to the uttermost. Christ is a personal Savior, but he redeems in the social and cosmic realms as well.

"...What think ye of Christ? Whose son is he?" (Matthew 22:42).

The answer of the Christian faith is that Jesus, as Christ, is Lord and Savior.

Bible Reading: Matthew 16:13-20

Jesus inquired of his disciples concerning his identity. He explored with them the various titles people had ascribed to him. Some speculated that he was John the Baptist, Elijah, Jeremiah, or one of several prophets. Then Jesus raised a more personal question. He asked, "But who do you say that I am?" (V. 15, RSV). Peter's response was quick and forthright: "You are the Christ, the Son of the living God" (v. 16, RSV). The praise that came from Jesus was equally forceful. Jesus indicated that Peter's confession came from divine revelation. He went on to assert that the church to be established and withstand all opposition from evil would be built on the truth of the confession that Jesus is the Christ (vv. 18-19).

Study Questions

1. What is the difference between an example and a savior?
2. Why does sinful humankind need a savior?
3. How do you understand Christ as liberator and reconciler?
4. What did the early Christians mean by the lordship of Christ?
5. What is the importance of the belief in the divinity of Christ?

Scripture References for Additional Study

Isaiah 45:14-23

An exclusive claim.

Isaiah 53

A disturbing appearance.

Ephesians 2:11-22
A radical result.

PART II
CHRISTIAN BELIEFS INTERPRETED

Chapter 16
The Coming of Christ

"He was in the world; but the world, though it owed its being to him, did not recognize him. He entered his own realm, and his own would not receive him. But to all who did receive him, to those who have yielded him their allegiance, he gave the right to become children of God..." (John 1:10-13, NEB).

Word Study

advent - arrival or coming into being.
incarnation - to embody. Jesus Christ is believed by Christians to be the very embodiment or enfleshment of God. Incarnation is central to Christianity.
Gentile - in New Testament time Gentiles were all non-Jews. They were not subject to Jewish law, especially regarding circumcision.
lost - in the biblical sense, those who are unsaved-the unconverted or those who have not experienced forgiveness of sins.

The coming of Christ is a most important event for all Christians. His coming splits our history. This happening is referred to as the Advent or "arrival." According to the calendar of Christians, Advent begins four Sundays before Christmas. But the coming of Christ has a special meaning in theology. Here his coming is understood as incarnation, which means embodiment or enfleshment. God enters history in Jesus Christ. Through the coming of Christ, God confronts us where we live our lives. We are at the center of our faith as we discuss the "Word made flesh."

It comes as a surprise to many Christians that the Gospel writers say so little about the birth of Christ. We are limited to the first two chapters of Matthew and Luke for what we know about Jesus up to his baptism, which introduces his ministry. In contrast, Christians often have much to say about his birth and even enter into dispute over it. Perhaps who Jesus became to the Gospel writers overshadowed any extensive concern about birth stories.

We should note that Mark and John omit entirely the account of his birth, while Matthew and Luke appear to have different reasons for relating the birth accounts. The details as set forth in these two accounts differ also. Matthew, as a Jew, was concerned that Jesus should be closely associated with Israel's history. Thus, Jesus' lineage is traced back through David to Abraham. He was born in Bethlehem, the city of David, and was said to be David's son. His coming fulfilled Old Testament prophecy. Luke, on the other hand, being a Gentile, was more concerned that the ancestral line of Jesus should go back beyond Abraham to Adam. Luke, a historian and the physician of the apostle Paul, was the apostle to the Gentiles and considered it essential that Jesus should be known as Savior of all humans, that is, of all the children of Adam and Eve. In both Matthew and Luke there is a movement from promise in the Old Testament (in the Law and the Prophets) to fulfillment in the coming of Christ.

It is important, however, that we be aware that Jesus came to seek and to save the lost. He did not come to destroy the Old Covenant but to fulfill it. Far beyond anything we may say about his birth is the real meaning of his coming. He came to bring light and life to all humans. His coming was not only an arrival; it was a saving event. It is in and through Jesus as the Christ, that God does his saving work among humans.

Bible Reading: Luke 2:1-32

The nativity (birth account) of Luke is very significant. The writer had appreciation for the Jewish roots of Jesus. The context of the birth narrative is a great outpouring of the Spirit through Mary and Zacharias (chapter 1). He puts John the Baptist clearly in the Israelite tradition. In the chapter of our focus Jesus was placed in the lineage of David (v. 4) and was appropriately born in Bethlehem. But Luke also elevated Jesus' birth to universal status. First he did so in the prophecy of Simeon (vv. 25-32) and then by presenting a genealogy that went back not to Abraham but to Adam (chapter 3). Luke's account of Jesus leads us to conclude that Jesus came to seek and save the lost. He makes no exception based upon race, sex, class, or nationality. He is the universal Savior.

Study Questions

1. What is the meaning of Advent? Explain.
2. How would you describe the incarnation?
3. Read the birth stories in Matthew and Luke. How do they agree? Differ?
4. In what way do the birth accounts illustrate the promise-the fulfillment scheme of revelation?
5. How would you sum up the deepest meaning of the coming of Christ?

Scripture References for Additional Study

Matthew 1:18-2:23

The birth of a king. Israel had the hope of a new age ruled over by "the Branch" (Jeremiah 23:1-8; Daniel 11:5-9; Zechariah 6:9-14). The Hebrew word for "branch" is the background to Matthew 2:23.

Galatians 3

Jesus Christ both divides and connects history.

PART II
CHRISTIAN BELIEFS INTERPRETED

Chapter 17
Ring In The Christ That Is To Be

Word Study

Socrates - acknowledged as the founder of Greek philosophy during the classical period.
grace - our unmerited or undeserved favor in the experience of salvation.
gratitude - a posture of thanksgiving in response to God's gift of salvation as well as for his benevolence in all of creation and history.
shepherd - one who tends sheep in a pastoral culture. The term is used to describe God's providential care of humanity. It is also used in reference to the minister's role as pastor of a congregation.
host - a favorite usage is in the twenty-third Psalm (v.5). The word is not used but the description is that of a host. The meaning is that God provides and comforts.

The time between Christmas and the New Year is very exciting for many people. It is a time of family reunion and visitation of friends and relatives. But isn't there also a message that this period brings to us and leaves with us? God has entered time through a babe, and history has been split by his birth. This happened at Christmas. Today the celebration of the birth of the Christ child is followed by the birth of a new year. What should this mean to us as Christians?

The coming of Christ means that a new era of salvation has dawned. "Grace and truth came through Jesus Christ," says

John in his Gospel. The New Year, then, after Christmas, is God's new age in which the Christ of God is to reign. Tennyson saw clearly this relation between Christmas and the New Year as he wrote:

Ring out the old, Ring in the new.
Ring happy bells, across the snow;
The year is going, let him go;
Ring out the false, ring in the true.

Ring in the valiant man and free,
The larger heart, the kindlier hand;
Ring out the darkness of the land,
Ring in the Christ that is to be.

After Christmas our future is vouchsafed in Christ. Our future is rooted in his future. We are secure in that faith. We like the apostle Paul, are assured that nothing "shall be able to separate us from the love of God, which is in Christ Jesus, our Lord" (Romans 8:39). "Our times be in his hands" and, therefore, if we trust God, we need not be afraid.

This is a good time for taking stock. Socrates was right: "An unexamined life is not worth living." Thus, between Christmas and the new year we ought to carefully assess our strengths and weaknesses in order that we may know how best to mend our lives. The one who was born on Christmas came to "seek and to save the lost." Christ's mission is to mend broken lives.

This is a good time to muse on God's purpose in this world. When an old year comes to its close and we are launched into an uncertain and unknown future, it is perhaps the best time to think about God's purpose unfolding in our midst. In spite of all evidence to the contrary, God is ruler yet.

Finally, this is a good time for thanksgiving. God extends his grace. He gives an unspeakable gift at Christmas time. God gave his "only begotten Son." Through him we may have eternal life. Our proper response to such generosity from God is gratitude. Our expression must be deeper than a mere "thank you." We must give our lives to him as the only adequate expression of our thankfulness.

And between Christmas and the new year we must remember what God has done for us throughout the year. Every blessing, large or small, must be part of our expression of gratitude. Thus, as the old year fades, let us ring into our lives "the Christ that is to be." God is our Shepherd and our Host.

Bible Reading: Isaiah 53

There is perhaps no other passage in the Old Testament that anticipates more vividly the passion and cross of Christ than this chapter. Almost every verse has a profound message. The passage speaks of the rejection, grief, and sorrow of the Servant of God. The Servant of God of this sublime chapter suffers vicariously for others. He is afflicted and oppressed. He is innocent in his suffering. The Servant is humble and obedient, even unto death. The Servant is an offering for sin. In his atoning death, the One takes upon himself the sins of many. Through that atonement he intercedes for the sins of many.

Study Questions

1. Why is the period between Christmas and the new year important for Christian reflection?
2. Can you connect the coming of Christ and the coming of a new year?
3. What do we mean by God's new age in Christ?
4. What are some of the things that we should think about at this time of the year?
5. How may we best express our gratitude to God at this time?

Scripture References for Additional Study

Genesis 3:20-21

Thought to be the first substitutionary sacrifice.

Genesis 21

A substitute for Isaac.

Exodus 12

A substitute for Israel.

Hebrews 4:14-5:10

A substitute for all.

PART II
CHRISTIAN BELIEFS INTERPRETED

Chapter 18
The Easter Message Today

"...as in Adam all die, even so in Christ shall all be made alive" (I Corinthians 15:22).

"...It is Christ that died, yea rather, that is risen again, who is even at the right hand of God, who also maketh intercession for us" (Romans 8:34).

Word Study

Easter - refers back to "Easter," goddess of spring. For Christians it is the culmination of God's plan of salvation. It is the day of the resurrection and is celebrated in view of the triumph of faith in Jesus Christ who overcomes sin and death.
redeemer - one who recovers, sets free, rescues, fulfills a promise, or compensates for. Literally from Latin *re* meaning back and *emere* meaning to buy; thus, to buy back. Jesus Christ is known as Redeemer in view of his atoning work for humans.
atonement - to set at one, to reconcile. Atonement is at-one-ment. It refers to satisfaction, reparation, expiation made for a wrong or injury. In the Christian sense it is the reconciliation between God and humans effected by Christ.
resurrection - from Latin *re* meaning again and *sugere* meaning to rise or to resurge; thus, to rise again, i.e., a rising again from the dead. Thus it is used to refer to the rising of Christ from the dead. It also is used in reference to the raising of Christians from the dead at the Day of Judgement.

death - the cessation of all vital functions of a living person or thing. Thus death is generally conceived as the extinction or the final destruction of life. But human expectations in religions and philosophies defy the finality of death. Such is the doctrine of the resurrection.

We turn now to the meaning of Easter. The God of the Bible is Creator, Redeemer, Judge, and Liberator. God creates humankind in his likeness for love and goodness. The world is said by God to be good. Humans are tempted to say no to God's commands, and we fall from God's favor. Because of our pride, self-will, and rebellion, we are in need of being redeemed, reborn, or re-created. The God of love desires an at-one-ment with us. To this end, God sent his Son into the world that we might be saved from sin and restored to a right relation to God.

The cross and resurrection climaxed God's saving work in Christ. All have died in the "First Adam," but Jesus Christ, the "Second Adam," comes as Savior of the sinful. The relation between the Old Testament (Covenant) and the New Testament (Covenant) is that of promise to fulfillment. From birth to death, from Bethlehem to Calvary, the mission of Jesus is the redeeming of sinful human beings.

The cross is the place where we meet the suffering of God. At the cross, the sinfulness of humanity is confronted by the holiness of God. The cross has two faces: one face is sin; the other is love. Faith enables us to see more than the shame and agony of the cross. The cross stands as the universal symbol of God's concern for human salvation.

The theme of the New Testament is the victory of life over death, of love over sin and evil. The Easter faith radiates throughout the New Testament. This is the reason why the early Christians selected the first day of the week as the day of rest and worship. The first day of the week (Sunday) was the day that God raised Jesus from the dead and made him both Lord and

Christ. Christian faith is resurrection faith. It is in the raising of Jesus from the dead that God reveals a love stronger that evil, sin, and death. The faith that Jesus is the Son of God brings the victory that overcomes the world.

Bible Reading

In this passage Paul stated in a most profound manner his doctrine of the resurrection. He placed in perspective the death and resurrection of Jesus Christ and indicated how the redemption of God through Christ centers on the faith in the resurrection. The resurrection, according to Paul, is the foundation of saving faith. The efficacy of preaching, the validity of faith, the assurance of salvation and the hope of a future life, all depend upon the fact of the resurrection. There is a triumphant affirmation (v.20) that Christ is risen. Paul exchanged the question mark of the doubters into an exclamation point for the faithful.

Study Questions

1. Discuss human sinfulness and the need for salvation.
2. Is there a relation between the life, ministry, death, and resurrection of Jesus?
3. What is the meaning of the cross?
4. What would be our condition without the Easter message?
5. How does the Easter message relate to life today?

Scripture References for Additional Study

Job 19:23-27

The assurance of Job.

Ezekiel 37

A promise for Israel.

Ephesians 1:16-23

The power for those who believe.

PART II
CHRISTIAN BELIEFS INTERPRETED

Chapter 19
The Holy Spirit and Sanctification

"...ye know...how God anointed Jesus of Nazareth with the Holy Ghost and with power..." (Acts 10:37-38).

"But ye shall receive power, after that the Holy Ghost is come upon you: and ye shall be witnesses unto me both in Jerusalem, and in all Judaea, and in Samaria, and unto the uttermost part of the earth" (Acts 1:8).

Word Study

interpreter - one who sets forth the meaning of, elucidates, explains, renders understandable, or translates.
guide - to lead or show the way to, direct the movement or course of. A guide is one who has knowledge of a destination or goal and assumes the responsibility of leading others to a desired end (place, attainment, value, ideal).
quickener - one who gives aliveness and vitality to another person or thing. A life-giver, an enlivener.
Pentecost - a Christian celebration on the seventh Sunday after Easter. It commemorates the descent of the Holy Spirit upon the apostles. From the Latin *pentecoste* or the Greek *pentekoste* (fiftieth day). The day of Pentecost is also called White Sunday or Whitsunday.
comforter - one who brings ease or consolation, help, air or support.
strengthener - one who provides power, vitality, moral or spiritual ability or resources to realize desired goals or ends.

sanctification - the act of being set apart as pure or holy purpose; consecration. From the Latin word *sanctus* meaning holy. Sanctification, then, is the process of becoming holy.

The deepest spiritual needs of humans are met through the presence and power of the Holy Spirit. The Holy Spirit is "God present with us for guidance, for comfort, and for strength." The Holy Spirit is our Interpreter, Guide, Quickener, Life-giver, and Sanctifier. There is a great deal more we may say about the work of the Holy Spirit, but these observations will be adequate for our present purpose.

The Christian fellowship that we know as the church was born at Pentecost. The Church is a spirit-filled "togetherness" of believers in Christ. After the experience of the cross, the disciples had grown weary and faint-hearted. Even the witnesses of the resurrection had not totally revived them. It was with the downpouring of the Holy Spirit that they became "strong in the Lord."

As Christians, we are in need of someone to open up for us the meaning of the Scripture. Even though we honestly seek the will of God, the way is not always plain. The Holy Spirit leads us into the truth. This truth concerns ourselves, our brothers and sisters, our world, and most of all, the mind and will of God. Furthermore, as fallible and finite persons, we are often confused concerning the direction of our lives. We need guidance. It is not adequate to rely upon signposts-we need the assistance of a guide. We need to be led and shown the way that leads to life. The Holy Spirit is the Guide for our Christian journey.

The Holy Spirit is the fulfillment of Jesus' promise "to be with us" for those of us who did not know him in "the days of his flesh." The Holy Spirit quickens us to new life and gives comfort and strength for the Christ-like life. The Holy Spirit is known as Comforter, Strengthener, and the Life-giver. Without the presence and power of the Holy Spirit, the Christian life is not possible. As our Life-giver, the Holy Spirit bears fruit in our lives. In Galatians 5:22-23 (RSV) Paul says: "But the fruit of the Spirit is love, joy, peace, patience, kindness, goodness, faithfulness, gentleness, self-control; against such there is no law."

Thus, we may say that the Holy Spirit is the One who sanctifies. Sanctify means to make holy, for it comes from the Latin word *sanctus* which means "holy." Sanctification is a process of spiritual growth. It is an experience that continues as long as we live. It is not a degree of grace that is conferred once and for all times. When the experience of sanctification is understood in this static manner, the believer is led into a sense of false security concerning his moral and spiritual condition. He or she becomes self-righteous and takes pride in his or her own goodness. Sanctification is a rather humbling experience. It makes the Christian aware that by oneself he or she cannot do any good, that "all is of grace," and that without the help of the Holy Spirit, life is not full. It is, then, the Holy Spirit, the Giver of life, who leads us forward as we "grow in the grace and knowledge of God."

Finally, the Holy Spirit is the spirit that rested upon Jesus. Jesus, who is our Lord and Savior, is the bearer of the Spirit of God. The spirits must be "tried" to determine if they be of God. Only the Spirit who is associated with Jesus is God's Spirit. The Holy Spirit is the Spirit that "brooded" over the chaos at creation and that gave the prophets their utterances. The Holy Spirit was uniquely present in the life and ministry of Jesus. Jesus is the standard by which we recognize the presence and power of the Holy Spirit. Paul was right when he said, "The Lord is the Spirit." The Holy Spirit is that which provides comfort and strength for the Christian life. Like Jesus and the early Christians, a true believer is anointed with the Holy Spirit and with power. The Holy Spirit is the Interpreter of truth, the Guide, the Life-giver, and the Sanctifier.

Bible Reading: Acts 2:1-38

This is a passage concerning the surprising work of God through the agony of the Holy Spirit. Luke movingly described the outpouring of the Holy Spirit on that eventful day. The Holy Spirit fell equally upon all who witnessed this presence and power. The Holy Spirit was an overpowering presence. One of the most remarkable evidences of that presence was the effect upon the apostles.

Peter is a good example. Peter had been outspoken during Jesus' earthly life, but wavering and uncertain in faith as well. Faced with the reality of the cross, he denied his Lord. But now under the power of the Holy Spirit he preached with certainty and power. Peter was sure that the crucified and resurrected Christ had now sent the Holy Spirit to continue his saving work. Peter exhorted his hearers to repent, bc baptized, and receive the Holy Spirit. There is every evidence that under his preaching the Holy Spirit was outpoured and that many lives were changed in a new redemptive relation to God.

Study Questions

1. Describe the importance of the Holy Spirit in the life of a Christian.
2. Describe the role of the Holy Spirit as Interpreter and Guide.
3. Describe the Holy Spirit as Life-giver.
4. Describe the Holy Spirit as Sanctifier.
5. How may we recognize the Holy Spirit?

Scripture References for Additional Study

Genesis 1:1-2; 2:7

The Spirit gives life.

Zechariah 4

The Spirit empowers.

John 14:15-27; 15:26; 16:12-15

The Spirit instructs.

I Corinthians 2:10-16
The Spirit enlightens.

PART II
CHRISTIAN BELIEFS INTERPRETED

Chapter 20
Grace and Reconciliation

"But God, who is rich in mercy, for his great love wherewith he loved us, even when we were dead in sins, hath quickened us together with Christ, (by grace ye are saved;) (Ephesians 2:4-5)

"But grow in grace, and in the knowledge of our Lord and Savior Jesus Christ..." (2 Peter 3:18)

Word Study

grace - the freely given, unmerited favor and love of God.
pity - sympathetic grief or sorrow for the suffering or misfortune of others.
mercy - compassion shown toward an offender or enemy. It is a disposition to forgive or forbear, i.e., forgiveness.
intercede - to plead or act in behalf of one in need or trouble. To enter a cause as mediator; to restore a wholesome relationship between two separated or estranged persons or parties.
paradox - a statement that seems to be self-contradictory but which in reality expresses a possible and often profound truth.
repent - to feel sorry for a wrong action, attitude, or decision. To feel such remorse for a sin or fault as to change one's ways.
forgive - to cease to blame or feel resentment about an offense or offender. To pardon one of wrongdoing and seek to be reconciled or restored to an amicable relationship.

Grace is the overflowing bounty of God. It is bestowed without merit or worth. The word "grace" comes from the same root as "gratuitous." Grace, then, is God's gratuitous blessing of favor. All good things, such as food, health, and shelter, are manifestations of God's grace. All creation is the sphere of divine grace. The greatest display of grace is God's redemption of humanity through the saving work of Christ and the sanctifying work of the Holy Spirit.

Grace is denoted by the Greek word *charis*. This word is used in the New Testament. It originally meant joy. Even before New Testament writers employed it, *charis* had begun to acquire the meaning of unmerited favor. The word *charis* as Paul used it took on the meaning that it still has for Christians. Paul used the word "grace" to mean God's undeserved favor extended to sinful humans for their salvation or reconciliation. By reconciliation we refer to the mending of the broken relationship that sin has brought about between humans and God.

Grace is not pity. Pity involves a certain amount of contempt on the part of the person showing it in reference to the person receiving it. Pity is usually very casual. When one expresses one's pity for another, one cares no more about the other person. The *giver* is not behind the *gift.*

Grace is not the same thing as mercy. Mercy does not imply contempt, and for this reason it is closer to grace than pity. Mercy is extended to another without expecting something in return. Mercy is an example of a high-level human feeling. To show mercy is a vital expression of the Christian faith.

Whereas mercy may be ascribed to humans at their highest and best, grace is a gift from God. God is the giver of grace. We may ascribe graciousness to humans, but grace is of divine origin. Grace is *favor Dei* meaning favor from God. While anything coming from God may come by grace, it is especially true that the redemption of humans is by grace. Thus Paul could write, "By grace are ye saved..." (Ephesians 2:8).

The person and work of Christ is the gracious content of the word of grace. Jesus was aware that in his own person God's saving purpose for us was manifest. Reconciliation of humans to God was to be achieved by Jesus giving his own life on a cross. The passion of Christ makes sense only in view of his role as Redeemer. In Christ, God confronts sinful humanity with reality of saving grace. The message of the New Testament is word of the cross and resurrection. At-one-ment with God became a possibility through the reconciling work of Christ.

God was in Christ reconciling the world unto himself. Sin must be atoned for, blotted out, and covered. In and through Christ, God's grace comes to us to forgive and pardon our sins. God intercedes for us and makes amends for us through the power of Christ's resurrection.

Grace is a paradox (it appears to contradict itself) in our experience. The Christian life demands of us our very best. Christians must live as if perfection were possible in this life. We must not sin that grace may abound. We must seek to work out our salvation with "fear and trembling." Christians must work as if they were going to live forever and live as though they were going to die tonight. At the same time they must open up their lives to God for the work of divine grace.

After all, salvation requires that we repent and believe. It is not earned but bestowed. Faith in God is not real apart from the awareness that one receives daily the forgiving grace of God. Our spiritual growth in the knowledge and likeness of Christ depends upon the sanctifying grace of the Holy Spirit. The challenge of the Christian life is summed up in the New Testament in these words: "...grow in grace, and in the knowledge of our Lord and Savior Jesus Christ" (2 Peter 3:18).

Bible Reading

We are told that if we are in Christ, we are a new creature. We have experienced a new birth and are living a different life (v. 17). We have been reconciled with God through Jesus Christ. But more than this, we are called to a ministry of reconciliation (v. 19). We are Christ's representatives among others. God has expressed his saving grace in redeeming us from sin through Christ who knew no sin. It is because Christ has interceded for us that we experience the righteousness of God.

Study Questions

1. What is grace? Compare grace with pity and mercy.
2. Relate the person and work of Christ to the reality of saving grace.
3. What is reconciliation?
4. Describe the reconciling work of Christ.
5. Describe the paradox of grace in the experience of salvation.

Scripture References for Additional Study

Nehemiah 9:16-27
The limitless potential of grace.
Zechariah 11:4-17
The limited exercise of grace.
Ephesians 1:3-10
The lavish distribution of grace.
Titus 2:11-14
The life-changing power of grace.

PART II
CHRISTIAN BELIEFS INTERPRETED

Chapter 21
The People of God

"Simeon hath declared how God at the first did visit the Gentiles, to take out of them a people for his name" (Acts 15:14).

"Who gave himself for us, that he might redeem us from all iniquity, and purify unto himself a peculiar people, zealous of good works" (Titus 2:14).

Word Study

ascend - to mount or move upward gradually. Ascension commemorates the ascending of Christ from earth to heaven. The commemoration takes place on the fortieth day after Easter.
fellowship - a community of interest, feeling, or belief. It is an association of persons having similar interests. The gathered congregation of believers in Christ is an intense form of fellowship.
organization - a group of persons united to form a whole-for action, worship, and service.
organism - a living creature or plant. An organism is alive, dynamic, and subject to growth. The church is true when it is a fellowship of love and is filled with the presence and power of the Spirit. The church is the true church when it is fulfilling its mission in the world.

The church, which was born as the result of the cross, resurrection, and ascension of Jesus, came to full strength after Pentecost. At the Jerusalem Conference held between the so-called "pillar apostles" (Peter, James, and John) and the apostles for the Gentiles (Paul and Barnabus), a very important decision had to be made. The question had to be answered as to whether those other than Jews could be admitted to membership in the church. The issue still is a live one; the question now is whether members of a certain race, class, color, or nationality are worthy of membership.

It was Paul's understanding that the church, which has Jesus Christ as its head and which is a spirit-filled community, is universal. The new Israel is an *open* fellowship, whereas the old Israel was a *closed* affair. All people are eligible for membership in the Christian church upon presenting the proper moral and spiritual credentials. These requirements have nothing to do with race, class, color, or nationality.

The church is the fellowship of the Spirit. It is a creation of the love of God and is thus known as a fellowship of love. The household of God is "the house that love built." This is God's design for the church in spite of disorder, disunion, and unbrotherly and unsisterly conduct. It is essential, therefore, to distinguish between the visible and invisible aspects of the church. There are some that hold membership in the visible institutional church that *do not* belong to the invisible heavenly fellowship of believers. Conversely, there are some that hold membership in the invisible church that do not belong to the visible. When we consider the fact that the visible church is the organ or instrument through which God does the saving work among humans on earth and that humanity is by nature in need of fellowship, church membership becomes very important. We should always bear in mind that a true church is not an organization or social club. It is an organism or fellowship. The visible church is not its really but may serve its well-being only when it is true to the purpose of the true church.

The "new birth," which alone makes one worthy of membership, is rooted in the Easter message-that is, in the meaning of the cross and resurrection. The Easter faith is the basis of our personal and collective faith and hope as members of the church. The church, as the people of God, is rightly called the body of Christ. Allowing for the many talents, gifts, members, and branches of the church, we must always be mindful that Christ alone is Head and that he is the source of its life.

"The Church's one foundation
Is Jesus Christ her Lord...
With His own blood He bought her
And for her life He died."

Bible Reading: Acts 15:1-31

This was an important event in the early days of the Christian Church. The issue to be decided was whether salvation was for the Gentiles. Were Gentiles to be circumcised in order to become Christians? It would appear that this was a male-oriented question. Since sexism was not their issue, we only mention it in passing.

Paul and Barnabas reported their success in evangelizing in Gentile territory (vv. 1-4). It was the Pharisees who first raised the concern for circumcision (v. 5). Since the Jerusalem congregation was made up of converted Jews, the issue caused real concern and cast doubt upon the work of Paul and Barnabas.

It is significant that Peter, as a result of a vision that had changed his mind toward inclusiveness, spoke out forcefully in favor of the Gentile mission. He recalled how God had been impartial with his saving grace and the outpouring of the Spirit (vv. 7-11). Peter was followed by James who also urged that the work continue (vv. 13-21).

The result was that a letter of greeting was sent by the Jerusalem assembly to the churches in Antioch and Syria. Paul and Barnabas were approved as chief representatives for the church in Gentile regions. Judas and Silas were sent to deliver the letter and to stabilize the situation. While the letter did indicate that circumcision would not be required of Gentiles, it did warn against other sins. Gentile Christians were to abstain from meats offered to idols, from blood, from things strangled, and from fornication (v. 29). The gospel was contextualized for the new situation.

Study Questions

1. Why do we refer to the church as the people of God?
2. What was the nature of the Jerusalem Conference?
3. What was Paul's general understanding of the church?
4. What is the importance of the difference between the visible and invisible church?
5. Relate the Easter message to the Christian understanding of the church.

Scripture References for Additional Study

Deuteronomy 4:15-24

The people claimed by God.

Hosea 1:2-2:1

The people reclaimed by God.

1 Peter 2:4-10

A task to be claimed by the people of God.

PART II
CHRISTIAN BELIEFS INTERPRETED

Chapter 22
Bread and Wine and Water

"He took bread, and gave thanks, and brake it...Likewise also the cup after supper..." (Luke 22:19-20).

"Then cometh Jesus from Galilee to Jordan unto John, to be baptized of him" (Matthew 3:13).

Word Study

sacrament - a rite believed to possess a sacred character. It is derived from the Latin word *sacrare* meaning to consecrate. Any sign or token of a solemn covenant or pledge.
symbol - a material object representing something else, often something abstract or spiritual (from the Greek words *syn*, meaning together, and *ballein,* meaning to throw; or to "throw together"); a symbol is something chosen to represent something else.
initiation - the act of beginning, commencing, or originating. It refers to the process of being admitted to membership in an organization, fraternity, or cult. One is instructed in the fundamentals or is ritually admitted to the organization.
Passover - a Jewish feast commemorating the night when God, smiting the firstborn of the Egyptians, "passed over" the houses of the children of Israel.
purification - from the Latin words *purus*, meaning pure, and *facere,* meaning to make. Thus it is to make pure or clean from foreign or debasing elements, i.e., to be made pure from sin.

ordinance - from the Latin word *ordinare*, meaning to set in order. A religious rite or ceremony. Some Baptists make much of the distinction between ordinance and sacrament and see the former as the only appropriate word.
baptism - from the Greek word *baptismos,* meaning immersion. Baptism is an initiatory or purifying experience, i.e., initiation into the church.
eucharist - from the Greek words *eu*, meaning well, and *charizesthai*, meaning to show favor. Consecrated bread and wine for the ordinance or sacrament of communion.

These simple elements of our daily life are sacramental symbols of our faith. In a sacrament a material and visible symbol represents an invisible grace. Bread and wine are served at the Lord's Table, and the member is admitted into full fellowship as he or she partakes of the initiation in the waters of baptism.

There are a number of approaches to the meaning of the sacraments. Many differences center around the manner of Christ's presence in the sacraments. Whether the church is conceived as a body (a collective or corporate unity) or as an individual affair based upon loose covenant ties between members is related to the role of the sacraments, and hence the importance ascribed to them.

The Lord's Supper, composed of bread and wine, is at the center of Christian worship. These elements are also used in the Passover feast. They have a time-honored meaning. Of the elements employed in the remembrance of the Exodus experience of Israel from Egyptian bondage, two have been lifted up by the Christian faith as useful. They are the unleavened bread and the fruit of the vine. It was characteristic of the early Christians to reinterpret words and symbols and give them new meanings.

The bread was given a special meaning by our Lord when he pointed it out as a symbol of his broken body. The cross was to be a place of physical suffering of our Lord. On the cross he experienced the depths of human pain. The most brutal attacks that evil and sinful humanity could inflict upon him were evident. The wine represents what he called "my shed blood." Wine, then, points to his suffering and death.

Sin and evil must be atoned for if they are to be overcome. At-one-ment with God is possible only if God, out of suffering, takes steps to make possible humankind's reconciliation. The Christ who died on a cross, who is raised from the dead, and who is with us always, meets us at his table. He sups and abides with the faithful. Through Holy Communion we cultivate his presence and remember his suffering and death for "us and salvation." "For as often as you eat this bread and drink the cup, you proclaim the Lord's death until he comes." (1 Corinthians 11:26). Let us keep the feast!

Water is an element of cleansing and purification. In Christian usage, baptism symbolizes dying to sin and being raised to newness of life. Baptism is not a process whereby one is saved. It is rather a dramatic demonstration that one has already experienced the new birth. It is a rite of initiation into the fellowship of believers in Christ. The change of life having already taken place, baptism becomes the sign and seal of the new life in Christ. The Christian faith is nurtured as we partake of these two sacraments instituted by our Lord. He was baptized in the Jordan River, and he instituted Communion during his Last Supper with the disciples on the night of his betrayal. Through the Lord's Supper we remember his death suffering and through the waters of baptism we indicate that we are dying to sin and are raised to newness of life. Thereby we are full members of the fellowship of believers in Christ.

Bible Reading: Matthew 3:1-17; Luke 22:7-20

The account of the baptism of Jesus is important for the Christian understanding of this rite. His forerunner, John the Baptist, baptized Jesus in the Jordan. John referred to the greater baptism that Jesus would bring, that is, baptism with the Holy Ghost. But Jesus submitted himself to baptism by John. John felt unworthy to baptize Jesus and appeared not to understand why it was to be so. John baptized sinners (Matthew 3:6, 8, 11), but Jesus, the sinless One, had no need to be baptized. Jesus, however, insisted that it be done to "fulfill all righteousness" (Matthew 3:15). The baptism took place with divine approval. There was a manifestation of the Godhead in view of this baptism. God invoked a blessing and the Holy Spirit descended upon Jesus in the form of a dove. Not only was the Son baptized as an example for all Christians but also the triune God approved and blessed the rite of baptism. Surely all this established baptism as an important ceremony for the Christian and the church.

There is a similar biblical warrant for the Lord's Supper. It was the time of year for the Jewish Passover. Jesus requested his disciples to locate a suitable place to observe the Passover. They found a large upper room and readied it for this time-honored meal. When the group was seated, Jesus indicated that he anticipated his suffering on the cross (Luke 22:15). He indicated that this would be his last opportunity to eat and drink with them until they were reunited in the kingdom of God.

Jesus took two elements from the Passover and invested them with great meaning. He selected the unleavened bread and the fruit of the vine. The bread symbolized his body to be broken, and the cup represented his blood to be shed. He made it clear that this was to be a memorial to his atoning death for human sin. It was a ceremony to be repeated from time to time in his memory until the kingdom comes.

Study Questions

1. What is a religious sacrament?
2. Discuss the origin of the two Protestant sacraments.
3. What does each mean?
4. Why are they at the center of Christian worship and experience?
5. Why should Christians partake of the sacraments today?

Scripture References for Additional Study

Romans 16:1-4

The finality of baptism.

1 Corinthians 11:17-34

The fellowship at the Supper.

PART II
CHRISTIAN BELIEFS INTERPRETED

Chapter 23
The Christian Lifestyle

"There is therefore now no condemnation to them which are in Christ Jesus, who walk not after the flesh, but after the Spirit" (Romans 8:1).

"If we live in the Spirit, let us also walk in the Spirit" (Galations 5:25).

Word Study

mediate - to settle disputes or to act as intermediary between parties.
perfection - having all the desired qualities; a completed action or state. *Perfectible*, on the other hand, refers to that which is capable of becoming or being made perfect. *Perfectionism* is the state of being perfect.
righteous - that which is good, proper, or just. *Unrighteous* is the opposite. It refers to the morally wrong or sinful. *Self-righteous* refers to a posture of being both strict in regard to moral standard and proud and self-justifying in one's attitude or status.
oppression - the act of subjecting the weak to the pressure of an unjust or harsh exercise of authority, privilege, or power. This is often matched by a feeling of being cast down on the part of the victims of the oppressive person(s) or power(s).
principle - a general or fundamental rule or truth on which others are based. From the Latin word *principum*, meaning a

beginning. Thus a principle is a basic truth, law, value, or rule of conduct as a primary source for other things based upon it.
structure - from the Latin word *structus,* meaning to build. A structure is a combination of related parts. It refers to the position or arrangements of these parts into a whole, i.e., an organization or society. Since persons exist in relation to other persons, we are becoming more and more aware that evil as well as good results in a structure to be reckoned with.

The Christian's style of life is bound up with the grace and forgiveness that come through Jesus Christ. He is the one who mediates between God and humans to overcome the brokeness between God and humans and between one person and another. God was in Christ reconciling the world unto himself. Sin has also produced a brokeness in the inner life. This too must be overcome through saving grace.

The Christian is called upon to be holy, as Christ is holy. A Christian is to live with the example of Christ as the model or pattern of living. What do we mean by a holy life? Does holiness mean that one has arrived at the spiritual goal? Does it mean that one is doing one's very best but is still seeking the truth and growing in grace? If we believe that we have already obtained our goal, then we hold a *static* view of the Christian life. On the other hand, if we hold that we are growing in the grace and knowledge of Christ, we have a *dynamic* or *progressive* understanding of the Christian life.

A holy life may be said to be perfectible in the sense that we are moving in the right direction and doing our level best. But it is not a perfectionism in which one reaches a self-righteous state.

The Christian life is beset with many perils. We are tempted to be lost sons and daughters (unrighteous) or elder brothers and sisters (self-righteous). We may become proud of our humility by thinking of the holy life in terms of piety and ritual. On the other hand, we may keep the Commandments and help the needy and thereby reckon our righteous behavior (our good works) as adequate for our salvation. We may think of the Christian life as the sum total of dos or don'ts. Some Christians speak mainly of what they don't do and thereby forget that the Christian life is affirmative. The holy life is an experience of spiritual and moral growth. It is to experience sanctification in which one seeks to press forward toward the "mark of the high calling of God in Christ Jesus" and to overcome both sins of commissions (those things we have done that we ought not to have done) and sins of omission (those things that we ought to have done that we have failed to do).

There can be no separation between *root* and *fruit* in Christian life. Faith and morals are related as good seed and good ground are related to an abundant harvest. The Christian (laity or clergy) is called to a life of witness and service. The Christian is called to where the action is-not because the cameras are there, but because our Lord is there among the poor, anxious, oppressed, and lonely.

Jesus has not presented us with a foolproof blueprint for the Christian life. He has provided us with principles to be applied to life situations that require decision and action. We are called to the Christian style of life here and now. Through Jesus' teaching, ministry, life, death, and resurrection, we are reminded that as someone has said "He was not crucified on an altar between two candles, but in the marketplace between two thieves."

We are reminded that we are by nature *social*-we seek human fellowship. Sin and evil are organized. Where there is a structure of evil there must likewise be a structure of grace to overcome it. We are called to a personal Christian style of life. We are at the same time members of a worldwide fellowship of those seeking to make life more human as well as more moral and spiritual. Furthermore, this fellowship is visible (earthly) and invisible (heavenly), local and universal, past, present, and future. The Christian style of life involves at once the *communion* of saints and the *cooperation* of the saints.

Bible Reading: Galatians 5:22-26

This entire chapter is good instruction for the Christian life. I have selected the verses listed because they provide a convenient summary of what is called "the fruit of the Spirit." This summary of virtues is a good description of the lifestyle of Christians. What a worthy list: love, joy, peace, long-suffering, gentleness, goodness, faith, meekness, and temperance. We are told that these belong to one who has "crucified the flesh." Furthermore, the Christian is said to be one who lives and walks in the Spirit. One who would like the Christian life should think on these things.

Study Questions

1. What is the basis of the Christian style of life?
2. Describe the holy life and the meaning of perfection?
3. Discuss some of the perils of the Christian style of life.
4. What is the relation between faith and morals?
5. What is the social aspect of the Christian life?

Scripture References for Additional Study

Psalm 1

A recipe for constant growth and a reminder about possible death.

James 2

The weakness of "one-legged" faith.

1 Corinthians 13

A lesson about Christian character.

PART II
CHRISTIAN BELIEFS INTERPRETED

Chapter 24
"In the End, God!"

"If a man die, shall he live again?..." (Job 14:14).

"For he must reign, till he hath put all enemies under his feet" (1 Corinthians 15:25).

"God shall wipe away all tears from their eyes; and there shall be no more death..." (Revelations 21:4).

Word Study

mortal - from the Latin words *mors* and *mortis*, meaning death. A condition of being subject to death. Refers to life that is finite or limited in potential and physical endurance. Life as lived in this present world.
holistic - same as "whole." Something which contains all the parts to make up a total entity. Full, intact, complete, healthy.
soul - unique theological meaning. It refers to the moral or spiritual part of a human being or the divine principle of life. The philosophical meaning of the Greeks held to the immortality of the soul but stressed its rational aspects.
body - the physical part of a human being, animal, or plant. A distinct mass or portion of matter or physical substance.
hope - to desire with expectation of fulfillment. It means to wish or want, but with confident expectation.

In spite of sin, evil, and death, the Christian lives in the assurance that God has the last word. While the Christian life is to be manifest here and now in life, witness, and service, it has a future dimension also. The Christian answer to Job's question is "Yes!" The Christian hope is rooted in the resurrection of Christ.

The Christian faith shares with humanity's earliest religious belief, the longing for survival after death. Humans have always wanted to believe that physical death is not a final "No!"

Another aspect of the Christian doctrine of the last things was borrowed from the Greek idea of the soul as immortal (not mortal or subject to physical death). The Hebrews did not appear to have a well-developed understanding of the future life until after they made contact with the Persians and the Greeks. The Hebrews, however, had a holistic (unified) idea of soul and body. The Greeks, on the other hand, understood soul and body to be separate. The body was considered to be mortal, the soul to be immortal. According to the Greeks, the body was a prison or hindrance to the soul, which belonged to the spiritual world. The early Christians combined the Hebrew and Greek ideas into a new outlook.

Paul, in 1 Corinthians 15, revealed both influences. He was trained as a rabbi in Jerusalem and as a Greek scholar in Tarsus. He spoke of two types of bodies-*sarx*, meaning body of this death, and a *somatic* body, which he calls "the temple of God." For Paul death is "the wages of sin" experienced in the body (sarx), but the somatic body it to be presented as a living sacrifice. All humans die in the "First Adam." All are made alive in the "Second Adam."

Perhaps the most crucial statement of the Christian doctrine of last things is found in the Corinthian passage mentioned above. Here Paul, though informed by the Greeks, rejected the idea of disembodied spirits. As a person rooted in Hebrew thought, he could not accept the existence of the soul *without* a body. He discussed earthly bodies and heavenly bodies and concluded that in the future life, the soul will dwell in a heavenly body. The soul, according to Paul, must have a body suitable to its environment. This means that Paul believed in the resurrection of the *body*, but not in the resurrection of the *flesh!*

The most important contribution of Paul is the tie he established between the future life and the resurrection of Christ. He declared that if Christ is not risen, then those who have died have perished. But because God has raised Jesus and made Him both Lord and Christ, death has no sting and the grave has no power. Man's eternal hope is bound with the resurrection.

The future life should not be conceived in terms of a place or a time but as a relation. This life is not an experience of quantity but of quality. As John in his Gospel put it, "to know God in Christ is eternal life." Eternal life is a new kind of life. According to Paul, it is a life "hid with Christ in God" (Colossians 3:3). It begins in the new birth. It is a present possession as well as a future hope. Paul could say, "For me to live is Christ, to die is gain" (Philippians 1:21).

Death has no power to hurt those who are with the Lord. God shall wipe away all tears from their eyes" (Revelation 7:7). Heaven is an everlasting saving relationship with God; hell is eternal separation from God. Heaven and hell are states of being, not geographic locations. Eternal life that is hid with Christ in God has no end. Nothing in this world or in the world to come can "separate us form the love of God, which is in Christ Jesus, our Lord (Romans 8:39).

"In the end, God!"

"The grace of the Lord Jesus Christ, and the love of God, and the communion of the Holy Ghost, be with you all. Amen" (2 Corinthians 13:14).

Bible Reading: Revelation 19:1-9

This chapter of Revelation is filled with the praise and adoration of God. God has conquered all foes and has realized God's redemptive purpose in all history and all of creation. God is seated upon the throne in heaven. All his servants praise him. Likewise all of creation acclaims God's triumph (the waters, the thunder, v. 6). The church triumphant prepares for its summing up of all things in God. In the end, God! "Alleluia: for the Lord God omnipotent reigneth" (v. 6).

Study Questions

1. What are the non-Christian contributions to the doctrine of last things? Explain.
2. What are the two meanings of the "body" in Paul's discussion?
3. Why do we say that Paul believed in the resurrection of the body but not in the resurrection of the flesh?
4. What is the tie between the Christian understanding of the future life and the resurrection of Christ?
5. Discuss the future life as *relation* rather than as *location*.

Scripture References for Additional Study

Psalms 15 and 24

Preparing for meeting the King.

Daniel 12:2-3; Matthew 25:31-46

The dividing of humanity.

1 John 3:1-3

The power of Christian hope.

Conclusion

Chapter 25

Our discussion began with a look at the foundations of Christian belief and closed with an interpretation of doctrines held by Christians.

The Bible is described as a source book for Christian doctrine. The Bible is taken seriously but not literally in this study. An attempt is made to introduce in concise form the necessary background to derive meaning from the Scriptures. The Bible is a living book in that it gives guidance for our lives today.

Theology deals with revelation-God's unveiling of his mind and will to us. The personal revelation of God in Christ is central to all that we know about God and his dealing with us. The Bible is the Word of God as it bears witness to God's revelation in Jesus Christ.

Theology as God-talk, as reasoning about God, must take the existence and nature of God seriously. We affirm that God is and that God is goodness, righteousness, love, and holiness *par excellence.* He is the source of that which is ultimate in being and virtue. God is a benevolent and provident God who creates, sustains, and redeems human life. He is Lord of history and the Author and Finisher of our faith.

Our view of humanity is realistic. We are sinners in need of redemption. We are rational and free. Human nature is a good thing spoiled. We have chosen a lower road when a better way is known and possible. Sin is the misuse of knowledge and freedom.

Jesus is our Savior. He came to seek and to save the lost. His life, ministry, death, and resurrection are tied to God's redemptive purpose and action for us and our salvation. Jesus as the Christ has appeared and done his saving work that we might be restored to a saving relation to God.

To this end of reconciliation with God, the Holy Spirit guides, comforts, and strengthens us. God's grace or undeserved favor is manifested in our hearts and lives. Salvation by grace is a gift, but we must respond in repentance and faith to God's generous offer before we may be reconciled to God. The experience of grace is a two-way street. God works, but we must respond with works of faith and love, toward God and toward humanity.

A Christian begins his or her life in Christ as a "babe" but grows to spiritual maturity. This is the meaning of sanctification. This growth is evident in the deepening of the inner life. This deepening relationship with God also expresses itself in human love. The Christian is called forth as "leaven" as "salt" and as "light."

We are by nature social, and therefore the church as a fellowship answers a need in both nature and grace. It is not good for humans to be alone. The church meets the human need for sociability, but it is not a social club. It is a fellowship of believers in Christ. The people of God enter into covenant with one another. They are called forth to witness and service in the world. The communion of the saints is fulfilled in cooperative worship and action.

The sacraments are visible signs of an invisible grace. They are the means whereby believers call to remembrance the beginnings of their faith and the saving deeds of their Lord. The Lord's Supper, baptism, and the preaching of the Word are a part of these experiences of devotion and reaffirmation of faith.

The Christian faith has much to say about the goodness of creation and the meaning and importance of personal life and human history. But the Christian's hope is not earthbound. Life continues beyond physical death, according to our faith. Eternal life is a new quality of life. It begins with conversion and develops toward maturity in the process of sanctification. The Christian's hope reaches beyond the circumstances of this life, for it is rooted in God. "In the end, God" sums up the triumphant note of the Christian faith.

Jesus is Liberator and Reconciler. The Christian faith is aware of sinful social structures. The context in which we live out our Christian lives is filled with evils that are collective as well as personal. We are exposed to anxieties, and we are assailed with various forms of oppression. Jesus is Liberator as he enables us to be more human and sets us free from the oppressive forces in our midst. He is Reconciler as he helps us overcome all estrangement's with other persons and ourselves and reconciles us with God.

Christian Beliefs Guidance

Christian Beliefs Guidance

A Word About the Guidance

The Guidance is written with the teacher of *Christian Beliefs* in mind. It is an additional resource that directs the teacher of the text toward serious reflection and continuing study. The commentary, questions for reflection, and the recommended reading all are designed for enlarging and deepening the understanding of the teacher/leader of the basic text.

While the text itself is a primer of theology, written by a minister-theologian for nontheologians, the Guidance provides opportunity for advanced study and critical reflection for all those involved in the Christian life and the church's ministry.

The work also includes an annotated bibliography for use by those who would like to pursue the study beyond the present volume.

Part I
Chapter I

Commentary

Our English word "Bible comes from the Greek word *biblos*, meaning book. The word comes from a word given to the inner pulp of the papyrus reed on which ancient books were written.

The Bible is divided into two sections known as the Old and New Testaments. The word "testament" was originally translated "covenant" and signifies the thought that each is a covenant that God made with his people. The Old Testament has thirty-nine; the New Testament, twenty-seven books.

The two testaments are subdivided into certain types of books. The Old Testament consists of the Law (*Torah*); Genesis,

Exodus, Leviticus, Numbers, Deuteronomy-these are sometimes referred to as the Pentateuch (five books); the Prophets, which consist of Former Prophets (Joshua, Judges, Samuel, Kings) and Latter Prophets (Isaiah, Jeremiah, Ezekiel, and the book of the Twelve-Hosea to Malachi); the Writings, which include the poetical books (Psalms, Proverbs, Job, Song of Songs, Ruth, Lamentations, Esther and Ecclesiastics); and Historical books (Daniel, Ezra, Nehemiah, and Chronicles.

The New Testament is divided into the Gospels (Matthew, Mark, Luke, and John); the Acts of the Apostles; the Epistles of Paul; the General Epistles; and the book of Revelation.*

*This material is presented in this fashion by Guy R. Duffield and N.M. Van Cleave in *Foundation of Pentecostal Theology*, published by L.I.F.E. Bible College, Los Angeles, California, in 1983.

The Bible is one book, but many different authors and editors wrote it over a period of more than 1,500 years. It is remarkable, therefore, to note the continuity of its message.

The word "canon" comes from the Greek work *kanon*, meaning a measuring rod or reed. It refers to a rule or standard. Thus the canon of the Bible consists of those books considered worthy to be included in holy Scriptures.

The writer considers the authority of the Bible as the standard for Christian faith and life. Its authority is due to the fact that God speaks savingly to us through the Bible. The Bible is to be read under the inspiration of the Holy Spirit. It is to be understood through our relation to Jesus Christ as the supreme revelation of God's will and word for us.

Questions for Reflection

1. What is the most important source book for Christians? Why?
2. What is the purpose of the historical study of the Bible?
3. What is the value of the literary study of the Bible?

4. Does the Bible contain a message from God? Explain.
5. What is the difference between the divine Word and the human words in the Bible?

Recommended Reading

Anderson, Bernhard W., *The Living Word of the Bible*. Philadelphia: The Westminster Press, 1979.
Fugita, Neil S., *Introducing the Bible*. Mahwah, NJ: Paulist Press, 1981.
Hestenes, Roberta, *Using the Bible in Groups*. Philadelphia: The Westminster Press, 1983.
Goodspeed, Edgar J., *How Came the Bible?* Nashville: Abingdon Press, 1976.
Turner, Nicholas, *Handbook for Biblical Studies*. Philadelphia: The Westminster Press, 1982.

Chapter 2

Commentary

The Word of God comes to us in human words. This is its strength and its greatest challenge. The fact that God has presented his saving revelation to us through human understanding gives it life and meaning in all places and among all people. The awareness that human words, as finite and fallible as they are, serve as a medium of communication poses a serious dilemma. But God can lift up anything in all creation and set it apart for a sacred purpose. This includes our words as it does our lives. The supreme illustrations of this truth is the incarnation, the Word made flesh.

Questions for Reflection

1. Why should the Bible not be worshipped or treated as an idol?
2. How do we relive the experience of the people of the Bible?

3. How does the revelation of God in Jesus Christ illustrate God's use of human to reveal the divine?
4. What do we mean when we say that the Bible contains the Word of God?
5. How do you understand the Bible as the living Word of God? Explain.

Recommended Reading

Anderson, Bernard W., *The Living Word of the Bible.* Philadelphia: The Westminster Press, 1979.

Chapter 3

Commentary

In the Old Testament, God is active in the life and history of a people. Thus by tracing the history of Israel we learn much about God's purpose for human life. It is through God's purpose as it unfolds in the collective personality of the people of the Old Testament that God speaks savingly to all humanity. But the Old Testament witnesses to God's encounter with individuals as well. God's revelation is often mediated through persons who are to exemplify and witness to the substance of the divine message to other persons and groups. In this way the living Word of God flows from the pages of the Old Testament.

Questions for Reflection

1. Discuss the "living" character of the Old Testament. What are some of its features?
2. How influential has the Bible been in shaping Western culture? Describe and give some examples.
3. Why do Christians look back from the New Testament to the Old Testament? Why is the Old Testament so important for Christian faith?

4. Why is the literary study of the Old Testament so important to its understanding? Illustrate.
5. How many religions of the world honor the Old Testament? How does each make use of the Old Testament?

Recommended Reading

Fugita, Neil S., *Introducing the Bible*. Mahwah, NJ: Paulist Press, 1981, Part I.

Goodspeed, Edgar J., *How Came the Bible?* Nashville: Abingdon Press, 1976, pp. 9-57.

Chapter 4

Commentary

The person and saving work of Jesus Christ are central to the understanding of the New Testament. In a real sense Christians read the Bible backwards. For Christians, the supreme revelation of God is the Word made flesh-God as revealed through Jesus Christ. Nowhere else is the mind and will of God made plain as it is in the incarnation. It is through this revelation that we come to know the message of the entire Bible. We also gain insight into the witness of the Holy Spirit, the direction for the Christian life, and the nature and mission of the church. All that is written in the New Testament bears witness to the central person of the Christian Faith-Jesus. It is in and through Christ that the message of the Bible remains alive and fresh as the news of each day.

Questions for Reflection

1. What does it mean to interpret the Bible in light of God's revelation in Jesus Christ?

2. What do Christians believe regarding the interpretation of the Old Testament in view of Jesus Christ? How does the centrality of Jesus Christ contribute to the unity of the biblical message?
3. What was Paul's main contribution to New Testament life and thought? Describe the nature and purpose of some of his letters.
4. Discuss the authorship, date, literary style, and message of the "Apocalypse of John." Why is Revelation so difficult to understand? Present briefly its vital message.
5. Does the Bible come directly from God without error? If the Bible has human authors who are imperfect, how can it be holy? How then is it the Living Word of God?

Recommended Reading

Anderson, Bernard W., *The Living Word of the Bible*. Philadelphia: The Westminster Press, 1979.
Fugita, Neil S., *Introducing the Bible*. Mahwah, NJ: Paulist Press, 1981, Part I.

Chapter 5

Commentary

Whenever the Christian faith is viewed from a historic perspective, tradition is an important consideration. As Christians affirm their personal and collective understanding of their faith, the witness of the faithful through the centuries takes on a valuable meaning. Those in the Free Church (the more informal church heritage) do not ascribe tradition with the depth of importance that the Roman Catholic and Eastern Orthodox churches do. But all mainline churches pay considerable attention to what Christians have confessed concerning their faith through the ages. All Christians place emphasis upon the memory of the church. The hindsight of the church is profitable for its future. We, therefore, prize the faith of the people of God in the Old Testament and the witness of Jesus, the apostles, saints, and ordinary believers. We caution, however, against being lost in the past. The tradition is to be our usable past. It is to be dynamic and it is to be worthy for future reference.

Questions for Reflection

1. Why is tradition so important for Christians? Why is it necessary to have a proper perspective on tradition?
2. How does the Sermon on the Mount illustrate the manner in which the past may come to life in the present? How does Jesus use the Law and the Prophets as a background for the gospel?
3. Describe oral tradition in the early church. Why did it last so long? How did the New Testament gain it special place? Explain the phasing out of oral tradition.
4. What are creeds, confessions, and dogmas? How should they be understood? What is their place in worship?
5. What is the importance of a thoughtful reflection upon the history of the church in relation to the message of the Bible?

Recommended Reading

Nelson, C. Ellis, *Where Faith Begins*. Atlanta: Knox Press, 1971.

Part II
Chapter 6

Commentary

Why should humans care if God exists? There are some people who insist that it does not matter if God exists or not. But, the study of humankind from prehistoric and preliterate times to the present indicates that concern for the existence of a divine reality has been persistent among human beings. There must be a reason for this.

I recently (summer of 1986) visited Tottori, Japan, overlooking the Sea of Japan. It was to this southern part of Honshu, the main island of Japan, that people came from the Korean kingdoms with their beliefs in Taoism, Buddhism, and Confucianism. They also held beliefs in divine beings. Belief in divine beings that portend the creation and well-being of human life was already present among the Ainu and the Shintoists. It illustrates that there is something inherent in human nature that longs for the divine. It also argues for the importance of the questions that Christians raise concerning the existence of God.

The existence of God meets a deep yearning and need at the heart of human life. It follows that the understanding of God is also important. The existence and character of the divine is so clearly tied together that early theologians such as Anselm argued that God is a necessary being. Existence is essential for the very nature of God. And, furthermore, God's existence is bound up with goodness and love. God exists beyond question, but that existence assures us of the abundance of goodness and love in all of creation and history.

One of the great questions raised by the existence of God as understood by Christians is the reality of evil. Not only Job but also Christians today are puzzled by the undeserved suffering of the righteous. Evil appears to be more than the absence of good. It is beyond human explanation and is a vital part of human experience. Our struggle against evil is a real fight. But why does evil *exist* as well as *persist* in a world believed to be created and sustained by a good and loving God? Would it not be better to accept the nonexistence of God? The answer is no. Without the existence of God our profoundest longing would go unanswered and we would not appreciate as completely the beauty and goodness of creation and salvation. The Christian faith as a whole does have a response to these questions. This will become more apparent as our discussion unfolds.

Questions for Reflection

1. Why does the existence of God linger so profoundly in human thought and faith?
2. What is the value of various proofs or demonstration for the existence of God? What do they accomplish?
3. Why is it essential to relate the existence and character of God?
4. Why is reflection upon the existence of God preferable to a blind leap of faith?
5. How does the problem of evil present a critical challenge to the existence of God? How do you come to terms with this issue?

Recommended Reading for Part II

Alves, Rubem, *I Believe in the Resurrection of the Body*. Philadelphia: Fortress Press, 1986.

Baillie, D.M., *God Was in Christ*. New York: The Scribner Book Companies Inc., 1948.

Bonino, Jose Miquez, *Doing Theology in a Revolutionary Situation*. Philadelphia: Fortress Press, 1975.

Cox, Harvey, *The Secular City*. New York: The Macmillan Publishing Company, 1965.

Cullmann, Oscar, *Baptism in the New Testament*. Philadelphia: Westminster Press, 1950.

Evans, Robert A. and Alice F., *Casebook for Christian Living*. Atlanta: John Knox Press, 1977.

Farmer, H.H., *The Word of Reconciliation*. Nashville: Abingdon Press, 1966.

Fowler, Jim and Keen, Sam. *Life Maps: Conversations on the Journey to Faith*. Minneapolis: Winston Press Inc., 1980.

Hellwig, Monika K., *The Eucharist and the Hunger of the World.* Mahwah, NJ, Paulist Press, 1976.
*Jones, William A., Jr., *God in the Ghetto.* Elgin, IL: Progressive Baptist Publishing House, 1979.
Kerans, Patrick, *Sinful Social Structures.* Mahwah, NJ: Paulist Press, 1974.
Lewis, C.S., *Mere Christianity.* New York: Macmillan Publishing Co., 1960.
McDonald, H.D., *Forgiveness and Atonement.* Grand Rapids: Baker Book House, 1984.
Manson, T.W., *The Servant Messiah.* New York: Cambridge University Press, 1961.
Niebuhr, H. Richard, *The Purpose of the Church and Its Ministry.* New York: Harper & Row, Publishers, Inc., 1977.
Pannenberg, Wolfhart, *Christian Spirituality.* Philadelphia: The Westminster Press, 1983.
Paul, Robert S., *Kingdom Come.* Grand Rapids: William B. Eerdmans Publishing Co., 1974.
Prenter, Regin, *The Church's Faith: A Primer of Christian Beliefs.* Philadelphia: Fortress Press, 1968.
Richardson, Alan, *Creeds in the Making.* New York: Macmillan Publishing Co., 1951.
Roberts, J. Deotis, *Liberation and Reconciliation: A Black Theology.* Philadelphia: The Westminster Press, 1971.
Robertson, E.H., *Man's Estimate of Man.* Atlanta: John Knox Press, 1958.
Russell, Letty M., ed,. *Changing Contexts of Our Faith.* Philadelphia: Fortress Press, 1985.
Smith, J. Alfred, Sr., *For the Facing of This Hour.* Elgin, IL: Progressive Baptist Publishing House, 1981.
Stegemann, Wolfgang, *The Gospel and the Poor.* Philadelphia: Fortress Press, 1984.

*Tracy, David and Cobb, John B., Jr., *Talking About God: Doing Theology in the Context of Modern Pluralism.* Minneapolis: Winston Press, 1983.
Wallis, James, *Agenda for Biblical People.* New York: Harper & Row Publishers Inc., 1984.
Williams, Daniel Day, *What Present-Day Theologians Are Thinking.* New York: Harper & Row Publishers Inc., 1952.
Winter, Gibson, *The Suburban Captivity of the Churches.* New York: Doubleday, 1961.

*Especially important sources for chapter 6.

Chapter 7

Commentary

The concept of personality as related to the nature of God is very important. It gives definiteness or specificity to the divine nature. Personality points to the personal dimension of human life as a point of reference. We are aware that personality is essential to our humanity. It is the thinking, feelings, and willing aspects of our nature. In ascribing personality to God, we are not diminishing God; we are exalting this dimension of our life.

God is the pattern of the personal. Personality of God is the source and standard of the personal in us. We are measured by the divine life. In this characteristic as in all others, God is independent and self-sufficient. We exist in a relationship of dependence. What independence we have is God-given. Thus, the personal life of God transcends the personal in our experience. God is the source and ground of personality in us. Thus, we point to personality in humans in its imperfect form in order to point immediately to personality in God as its source.

God is perfect personality, but God is not less than the highest expression of the personal in human experience.

Questions for Reflection

1. Describe the essential traits of personality as we know and experience them.
2. What difference does it make to conceive of God as personal spirit? Why not impersonal spirit?
3. How do we understand the personal in relation to God and ourselves?
4. Discuss mind, purpose, person, and spirit as you think of God.
5. Why is *communion* rather than *union* a proper way of describing a close relation to God?

Recommended Reading

Roberts, J. Deotis, *Liberation and Reconciliation: A Black Theology*. Philadelphia: The Westminster Press, 1971, chaps. 2-4.

Chapter 8

Commentary

The holiness of God is to be lifted up as an ethical attribute of God *par excellence*. Holiness refers to the purity of God's being. It is God's holiness that set him apart and above all else. It is a most characteristic virtue of God's true nature; holiness implies moral perfection.

Isaiah's vision is a biblical frame of reference for the meaning of holiness (Isaiah 6:3). The seraphims cry "Holy, holy, holy, is the LORD of hosts..." This captures the basic sense of the holiness of One who is ineffable and morally pure. When Moses was called by God from the burning bush, he was commanded to take off his shoes, for this was "holy ground"

(Exodus 3:5). An object, time, or place set apart for the presence or service of God was said to be holy.

There is perhaps no other attribute of God that says more about what separates God from us than this attribute. God's holiness represents moral perfection. It is that which sets the standard for our moral perfection.

Questions for Reflection

1. Put in your own words the meaning of "holiness" as applied to God.
2. Discuss what "holy" implies in our encounter with God.
3. Reflect upon the meaning we have derived from "holiness" in the personal life of faith as well as in our church traditions.
4. How do Isaiah and Moses help us to understand holiness in God?
5. In what way does holiness in God sum up that which separates humanity from divinity?

Recommended Reading

Roberts, J. Deotis, *Liberation and Reconciliation: A Black Theology*. Philadelphia: The Westminster Press, 1971, chaps. 3-4.

Chapter 9

Commentary

This is a period in human history when there is much concern about the dignity and rights of human beings. Christians ought to find their grounds for the just treatment of all persons in their faith. There are biblical warrants for the belief that God is the ultimate source of justice.

In a recent trip to the Far East, I was impressed that hotels had copies of both the Bible and the Teachings of Buddha.

As a student of religions, I read daily from both. But I was disappointed that only the New Testament was available. It was fortunate that I had with me an entire Bible. A Japanese friend told me that many Christian missionary groups stress only the New Testament. Reasons for this varied. But the sad truth is that many Christians do not stress the unity and totality of the biblical revelation. How then can they communicate the revelation of God's justice?

So much of what the Bible has to say about God's righteousness is found in the Old Testament that it is unfortunate to leave this out. Without the Exodus, the Law, and the Prophets, one does not have a proper basis to appreciate the understanding of God's righteousness in Jesus or Paul. It may be true that Christians read the Old Testament backwards, but they cannot fully understand their faith if they do not read it.

It is because we do not fully appreciate the full meaning of justice as an attribute of the divine nature that so much Christian witness is privatized. One should view the recent liberation theologies as a corrective to this lack. It is essential that we see this innovative movement as a new look at the biblical concept of social justice. We should not write it off as only Marxist social analysis. The justice (or righteousness) of God is essential to an adequate understanding of God as Christians know him.

Questions for Reflection

1. Define the biblical meaning of the righteousness in God.
2. Why has the concept of the righteousness of God assumed such great importance in recent years?
3. What happens to the meaning of this important attribute of God when Christians teach only the New Testament?
4. Why is the Old Testament so important in defining the justice (and/or righteousness) of God?

5. How would you relate being made righteous to being justified? How do we move from understanding the justice of God to personal salvation and then to "doing justly"?

Recommended Reading

Coste, Rene, *Marxist Analysis and Christian Faith.* Maryknoll, NY: Orbis Books, 1976, pp. 1-26.
Wallis, James, *Agenda for Biblical People.* New York: Harper & Row, Publishers Inc., 1984, chapter 1.

Chapter 10

Commentary

There are several meanings to the word "love." Our discussion attempts first to clarify the meaning of love as it is used biblically and theologically in reference to God. Thereafter, we understand its meaning as applied to humans in their relation to God and to one another. Love has a vertical reach to God. It has a horizontal reach from one person to other persons, and it has an introspective reach within its devotional, spiritual, and mystical dimensions.

In this chapter we are primarily concerned about the love of God or love as an attribute of God. We have observed that the most characteristic Hebrew word is *chesed*, meaning steadfast love. The most appropriate Greek term is *agape,* meaning self-giving love. The latter meaning is closely associated with grace. The grace of God (*favor Dei*) is his "unmerited favor." God is love. But God so loved the world that he *gave* his only begotten son so that sinful humans might be saved. God's love is demonstrated in self-giving salvific action for sinful humanity.

It is important that we keep in mind the coalescence of love with justice in God. Martin Luther King, Jr. often spoke of the tough-mindedness and tenderheartedness of God. This was his way of reminding us that justice as well as love is grounded in the divine nature. I have chosen to speak of God as One who is lovingly just. This union of love with justice in God has profound ethical, religious, and social significance.

Questions for Reflection

1. Discuss the Old Testament usage of *chesed*, especially in the book of Hosea and chapter 40 in the book of Isaiah.
2. What additional meaning do you derive form the word *chesed* as you define it as "covenant-love"? Does this meaning enrich your understanding of the character of God and his dealing with us?
3. Discuss the ethical, redemptive, and social significance of God's love.
4. How is the love of God closely related to God's grace?
5. How are love and justice in God related, and what is the importance of this relationship?

Recommended Reading

King, Martin Luther, Jr., *Strength to Love.* Philadelphia: Fortress Press, 1981.

Chapter 11

Commentary

The doctrine of the trinity is one that puzzles many Christians. It raises the question, How can three become one? Radical monotheism, whether Christian, Jewish, or Islamic, is challenged by this issue. If we believe profoundly in the oneness of God, the doctrine of the trinity, if reflected upon, does raise serious doubts in our minds. Is the doctrine as traditionally stated sufficiently important for the defense that it requires? I believe the answer is yes. But, at the same time, I do not believe that logic alone can justify it.

First of all, the doctrine is not a mathematical and logical problem to be solved. It comes out of the experience of Christians with God. Both the doctrine and the issues raised by it require a faith response, which is reasonable but not rational. It is based upon revelation to faith and not pure intellectual reflection.

Second, we need to observe how the doctrine of the trinity developed and how Christian thinkers and believers have interpreted it through the centuries. It was first expressed by the people of the Bible, mainly in terms of how they experienced through faith their relation to God. It is always to be understood in a redemptive sense. A saving relationship with God undergirds any meaningful understanding of the trinity. Thus, the Christian encounter with cultures outside of Palestine called forth reflection on the doctrine of the trinity that changed its form but not its substance. In recent times our knowledge of depth psychology as well as sociology has raised new issues. At the same time this new knowledge has possibilities of deepening our understanding.

We have already indicated how the understanding of human personality casts light upon the divine personality. The trinity has to do with the internal life of God as well as God's saving relationship to us. It follows that a profound knowledge of our highest and best selves portends a deepening of our knowledge of God. But this is true only in the light of a faith response to God's approach to us.

Finally, the trinity is important because it is the result of how God makes himself known to us for our salvation. The one God unveils his mind and will to us as Creator, Redeemer, and Reconciler. The more we understand regarding the Godhead and the internal relations with in, the more we know about the essence and very nature of God. This leads to a deepening of our understanding of the redemptive plan and the redemptive act on our behalf. The trinity expresses in a profound sense how God creates, redeems, and sanctifies. It is our God who does this as Father, Son, and Holy Spirit.

Questions for Reflection

1. Does the doctrine of the trinity present a problem for the belief in monotheism? How is it possible to reconcile this conflict?
2. What is the importance of the doctrine? What is the best way to discuss and explain the trinity?
3. Why has the doctrine of the trinity been expressed in different ways throughout Christian history? How does it retain its substance?
4. How does the trinity enable us to understand the internal life of the Godhead? Why is this important?
5. Attempt your own formulation of the doctrine of the trinity, with emphasis upon how God saves us.

Recommended Reading

Richardson, Alan, *Creeds in the Making*. New York: Macmillan Publishing Co., 1961, chap. III.

Chapter 12

Commentary

Human nature is central to any worthy reflection upon faith or ethics in the Christian perspective. Any reflection upon the redemptive content of the gospel must give due attention to the place of humanity within the divine purpose. But this concern for humans must be balanced by a concern for all of creation and all of history.

Feminist theologians have sensitized us to the need to use inclusive language and thoughts as we refer to males and females. It is no longer adequate to use "man" as a generic frame of reference. Women must be given their equal and rightful place in any adequate discussion of all human life. Thus, we have selected the word "humaneotology" to replace the traditional "anthropology" of theological textbooks. The language change is only symbolic of a shift in consciousness toward a more comprehensive liberation perspective for women as unique and precious in God's creative and redemptive purpose.

Environmentalists have likewise raised issues that should sharpen our perspective on the place of humans in a vast creation. The explosion of knowledge in the natural sciences, space travel and research, international communication, and even the nuclear threat of physical annihilation have sharpened our vision regarding the human situation. Christians must now reflect upon the place of humans in creation that sustains us but that may have its own rightful place in the divine plan. Does the whole creation exist only to fulfill human ends? What is the human responsibility to all of creation?

Finally, our perspective is enhanced by the insights of liberation theology. When we shift our focus in theology from human destiny to human dignity, new issues arise. Critics of liberation theology, who focus only upon the use of Marxist analysis by some liberation theologians, fail to see the challenge of injustices. Issues of human rights and liberation from oppression belong to the biblical agenda of social justice. There is no way to take the message of the entire Bible seriously without coming face to face with the Exodus, the prophets of social justice, and the Sermon on the Mount. Thus, questions of human dignity must be integral to an adequate humaneotology.

Questions for Reflection

1. What are some new considerations for a doctrine of human nature?
2. What are some of the issues raised by feminist theologians concerning this doctrine? Are they valid? Why?

3. Are the issues raised by environmentalists valid? Why do they question the placement of humans at the center of God's creation? How do you respond?
4. How do you understand the phrase "image of God"? How does this understanding help overcome the oppression of persons due to sex, class, or race?
5. If we understand human nature according to biblical references, what is the potential and intention of human life? How may these be realized?

Recommended Reading

Farmer, Kathleen, "Retelling the Story: Reinterpreting Biblical Tradition as a Woman" in *Changing Contexts of Our Faith*, edited by Letty M. Russell. Philadelphia: Fortress Press, 1985, pp. 49-62.

Chapter 13

Commentary

We are constantly beset with the reality of human sin within others and ourselves. There is no time or place where human beings are or have been that sin is not a reality. Sin is so universal and so omnipresent that we are capable of transforming every good as well as every potential good into something evil. Every time there is a breakthrough in science, we must immediately think of ways to keep the new knowledge from becoming a curse rather than a blessing. Human nature is itself a good thing spoiled. How can this be? God created human nature as a good thing, and yet we face on every hand the stark reality of human sinfulness.

Facing this reality is a challenge to our faith. The account of the Fall (Genesis 3) has traditionally been used to explain our estrangement from God's purpose for human life, and yet this account often raises many puzzling questions. It describes sin more than it explains the why of human sin. What is the place or role of God in this reality? Why is there this fault and propensity in human nature? What is the human guilt and responsibility in human sin?

The Fall account helps us describe what we experience as sin. It is appropriate that it follows the accounts of creation. Sin is indeed a curse of creation. That which has begun with a noble purpose experiences imbalance and disharmony. Estrangement from God, separation from self and others, destruction of the best within us-these results follow in the wake of sinfulness.

This awareness of human sin is foundational to evangelical faith. The fact of personal sin is essential to understanding human nature. Each person is faced with this reality. It must be confronted and dealt with. But even in the Fall story itself there is another reality, that is to say, the "sociality" of sin. Humans are social beings and we seek to draw others into a relationship with us for evil as well as for good ends. We seek community, whether it is good or evil. Thus an evangelical faith that is purely individual is inadequate. We must go on to deal with the social reality of sin.

I will mention only one other matter here. It has to do with understanding how humans, according to their nature, relate to the reality of sin. We are free and responsible beings. This explains to a large degree human guilt and responsibility for our sinful condition. The freedom to choose evil is equal to the freedom to choose good. Indeed, true selfhood appears to require both. God relates to us as persons. This relationship is one of love. Love can be expressed only when there is the quality of selfhood. It is always possible to say no to the God who creates and redeems us. It is God's desire that we say yes. When we do so, we find our highest fulfillment in a relationship of love, both human and divine. To this end, Christian faith assures us of divine aid.

Questions for Reflection

1. Discuss the universal reality of human sinfulness.
2. Why does sin appear to be a good thing spoiled?
3. Why is the reality of sin such a great challenge to our faith?
4. Why is the understanding of sin in evangelical faith so important? Why is it necessary to expand the evangelicals' traditional view of sin as merely personal?
5. Reflect on human freedom and responsibility in relation to a doctrine of sin. Are humans left alone in their struggle against sin?

Recommended Reading

Robertson, E.H., *Man's Estimate of Man.* Atlanta: John Knox Press, 1958, pp. 51-84.

Chapter 14

Commentary

Christians must make decisions concerning Jesus. It is possible to believe in the Christ of dogma without taking seriously the Jesus of history. An essential affirmation of the Christian faith has to do with the birth, life, ministry, death, and resurrection of Jesus. Thus, the focus on the Jesus who came and lived among humans is precious to the Christian faith and life.

This aspect of Christian theology has received much attention in liberal theology for many years. It was very much lifted up in the theology of the social gospel. There was a great decline of this in the middle of this century due to the ascendancy of Karl Barth and Rudolph Bultmann as dominant theological spokespersons. Though challenged decisively by Donald Baillie and Dietrich Bonhoeffer, Barth and Bultmann's view still held the field. This lack of emphasis upon the Jesus of history prevailed until the late sixties when various liberation theologies raised the issue of the vital importance of the Jesus who lived among humans. Their paradigmatic biblical text became Luke 4:18, where Jesus describes his mission as liberator of the oppressed. It is also important to note that the black church never abandoned the Jesus of history. The writings of Howard Thurman and Martin Luther King, Jr., among many others will support this.

This concern for a rediscovery of Jesus in the days of his flesh has taken on great emphasis by recent black theologians in the United States and by liberation theologians in Latin America. Indeed, it has unearthed much definitive evidence that the wretched of the earth have never given up belief in the humanity of God as demonstrated in Jesus' identification with the poor and oppressed as well as the sinful in need of forgiveness. The entire life story of Jesus is precious to those who seek deliverance from oppression as well as freedom over the powers of sin and death. Feminist theologians have likewise observed how Jesus related compassionately to the women who sought his help and forgiveness.

In a word, we would make the point that Christians need to come to terms with the Jesus of history. This alone makes a theology *incarnational.* Incarnation as we view it, is God entering creation in Jesus Christ. It is enfleshment-God with us in Jesus Christ under the conditions of the human situation. Thus, a theology can be *Christological* without being *incarnational.* We can believe in the Christ of dogma without taking seriously the Jesus of history. What will you do with Jesus?

Questions for Reflection

1. What is involved in placing special emphasis upon the life and ministry of Jesus? Why is it important to do this?
2. How did Christian theologians move away from the Jesus of history in favor of the Christ of dogma?
3. Who kept the belief in the life of Jesus alive?

4. What is the significance of the Jesus of history in liberation theologies?
5. What do we mean when we say a theology can be *Christological* without being *incarnational?* Should it be both? Explain.

Recommended Reading

Baillie, D.M., *God Was in Christ.* New York: The Scribner Book Companies Inc., 1948, pp. 9-54.
Bonhoeffer, Dietrich, *The Cost of Discipleship*. New York: Macmillan Publishing Company, 1963.
Stegemann, Wolfgang. *The Gospel and the Poor.* Philadelphia: Fortress Press, 1984.
Thurman, Howard, *Jesus and the Disinherited.* Richmond, IN: Friends United Press, 1981.

Chapter 15

Commentary

While some people have problems accepting the humanity of Jesus, others are equally disturbed by his divinity. This is not a new problem, for it was one of the decisive problems discussed early in Christian history. Any serious reflection upon a total Christological view must come to terms with what seems an insurmountable logical problem. It should be instructive that early Christians seemed to have accepted the belief that the same Jesus who dwelt amongst them in the flesh was in some sense with them after the resurrection. One need only read the book of Acts to discover that Peter and Paul were filled with this belief. It was their resource and driving power.

It was when Christians encountered Greek philosophy with its "either-or" logic that the matter became troublesome. In addition, they also met the doctrine of substance, which in Plato had made a radical distinction between material and immaterial substance. In fact, both the logic and metaphysics of Greek thought raised critical issues regarding how Jesus could be human and divine at the same time. Thus, the tools of the human mind then critically examine the simple belief in Jesus as "God with us". But the faith in the centrality of Jesus as God Incarnate was too central and dynamic to Christian faith to be shipwrecked on these human shoals. The essence of the Christian faith is revelation to faith.

Jesus is the Christ, the church decided. His divinity does not diminish his humanity. His humanity does not take away from his divinity. He is both human and divine. We have already stated reasons why his human life is important. On the other hand, Christians cannot give up his divinity. If we have only a human Jesus, we have a noble example in the moral sphere. But we are sinful human beings who are saved by grace. Christianity does not advocate self-salvation. We need a savior. It is God who saves us in Jesus as the Christ. Thus, we argue that the Jesus of history is the Christ of faith.

Questions for Reflection

1. What are the strengths and weaknesses in viewing Jesus only in human terms?
2. Why did the issue of the humanity and divinity of Jesus Christ develop to such a point of intensity?
3. How does sin and the need for salvation relate to how we understand Jesus as the Christ?
4. Reflect upon the sinlessness of Jesus Christ. How do you understand this? What is its importance?
5. What does it mean to say that the Jesus of history is the Christ of faith? It this a tenable position? Why?

Recommended Reading

Baillie, D.M., *God Was in Christ.* New York: The Scribner Book Companies Inc., 1948, chaps. III and IV.

Richardson, Alan, *Creeds in the Making.* New York: Macmillan Publishing Co., 1951, chaps. IV and V.

Chapter 16

Commentary

The focus here is upon the meaning of Advent. The season of Christmas is very sacred for Christians. We attempt to place due emphasis upon the birth of Jesus. This is to overcome the excessive commercialization of this holy season. The importance of this season goes beyond the usual family outings, the exchanging of gifts, and the festivities common to the event.

Christ himself is Christmas. What does this season really mean to Christians? The coming of Christ is significant in the manner of his birth. He had a lowly birth. His birth in a stable is symbolic of his identification with the disinherited. Shepherds, angels, glad tidings, wise men from the East, the Song of Mary, the prophecy of Zachariah-these and more indicate significance of his birth. His birth is more to be understood as to its meaning than as a particular date on the calendar. History itself takes on a new interpretation as a result of this birth.

Napoleon was reminded once that history would be the judge of his actions. He responded with his characteristic self-confidence. "I make history." Napoleon was wrong. But in the case of Jesus, a new aeon of history was born when he entered human time. History was divided by his birth. The chronology is not important. The quality of history and its redemptive significance are heightened and transformed by his birth. Henceforth, God's plan of redemption is fulfilled. God's promises are now complete. The Word is made flesh. God is with us. The cradle of Bethlehem is to rule both earth and heaven.

Again we are reminded that the Christian faith is *incarnational.* Creation is brought together with redemption. The God who created all things and pronounced the goodness of creation now selects the created order as a medium of redemption. Archbishop William Temple observed once that Christianity is the most materialistic of all religions because of the incarnation. The God who is the author of creation is also the giver of grace. God's unique, supreme, and saving revelation uses creation as its medium of expression.

Thus, as we exchange gifts at Christmas, we only celebrate the birth of the savior if we remember God's redemptive gift to us in Jesus Christ. John 3:16 sums it up best: "God so loved the world, that he gave his only begotten son that whosoever believeth in him should not perish, but have everlasting life."

Questions for Reflection

1. What is the real meaning of Christmas for the Christian believer? Do we usually give adequate attention to the significance of this event?
2. What aspects of the birth of Christ indicate his compassion for the poor and disinherited? Discuss.
3. How does the birth of Jesus give new meaning to history?
4. When we assert that the birth of Jesus brings creation and redemption together, what do we mean?
5. Discuss the meaning of John 3:16 in relation to our reflection upon the importance of the birth of Jesus and the real meaning of Christmas.

Recommended Reading

Thurman, Howard, *The Mood of Christmas*. New York: Harper & Row, Publishers Inc., 1971, pp. 31-118.

Chapter 17

Commentary

Christians should find the new year a suitable sequel to Christmas. If Christmas has to do with *faith*, the new year points to *hope*. We are reminded that we stand between two periods of human time.

As Christians we should have a special outlook on God's providence. We believe that all belongs to God. We believe that time and eternity are related. God has a purpose that is constantly unfolding and towards which all history and all creation move. Plato believed that time is the moving image of eternity. But Christians go even further, since history is a means through which God works out his saving purpose in the midst of time.

Christians are expected to examine carefully how they have lived during the past. We are also aware that we never fully measure up to what is required. In this regard we do our level best, and God by grace makes the measure full. We work as though we will live forever. We live as though we will die tonight. The new year is a proper time to estimate where we are in seeking to do the will of God.

We are aware that there are awesome social and structural evils in our midst. The evil of racism as institutionalized in South Africa seems insurmountable. The threat of nuclear war hovers endlessly around us. It is so foreboding that many young people have never known a future without the presence of this threat. I am told that some young people have so internalized this threat that they do not anticipate a life with a reasonable longevity. Drugs have become the scourge of our nation. Our future grows extremely dim as youth seem determined to self-destruct. These are just a few of the evils that make hope difficult and the future uncertain. But as Christians we continue to believe that God runs history. God is the God of the future, and we stretch out on his promises. We have biblical warrants and the testimony of history that God rules and overrules in human affairs as well as in a personal life of prayer and faith. We believe that the future belongs to God. Therefore, after all is said and done, our lives are in God's hands.

A Christian should, therefore, be prepared to face tomorrow. We are so sure of God's providence that we invest our best efforts in the tasks that we believe God sets before us. We must be up and doing. We are co-creators and co-laborers with God. God does much of the work in the world through humans who trust in God's purposes and who act upon his promises. We are neither completely optimistic nor completely pessimistic as Christians. We are "possiblists." We believe that many things are possible through God. Our future belongs to God. We move forward with the confidence of faith.

Questions for Reflection

1. How do you view the meaning of the new year in relation to Christmas? How should Christians link the two?
2. What is the relationship between time and eternity according to the Christian faith?
3. What are some important considerations as we examine our lives in the past and anticipate the future?
4. Discuss some social evils that threaten the future. Does it make any difference to see these through the eyes of faith in God? Explain.
5. What should be our involvement in God's future? How and why?

Recommended Reading

Baillie, D.M., *God Was in Christ.* New York: The Scribner Book Companies Inc., 1948, pp.71-79.

Thurman, Howard, *The Mood of Christmas.* New York: Harper & Row, Publishers, Inc., 1973, pp. 121-127.

Chapter 18

Commentary

The Christian faith finds its highest expression in the meaning of Easter. I stress the meaning of Easter rather than its celebration. Occasionally the worship and liturgy associated with Easter are worthy of the vital message that they represent, but too often the Easter season is given to materialism and even hedonism that are far removed from the meaning of the death and resurrection of our Lord and Liberator.

The real Easter garments are spiritual. They are not new dresses, hats, shoes, or suits. The proper Easter "clothes" are new hearts and new lives in Christ. The old garments of sin and death are discarded. These are replaced by faith, hope and love-the attire appropriate for the new birth. Easter clothes for the Christian are Christian virtues, such as long-suffering, meekness, love, faith, and hope.

The cross and resurrection must be closely linked. In fact, they cannot be separated. The Christian life is truncated if we accept the cross without the resurrection or the resurrection without the cross. If we accept the cross alone, we too easily glory in suffering, even unmerited suffering or suffering associated with injustices. We are not likely to be able to distinguish between redemptive and nonredemptive suffering. If, on the other hand, we embrace the resurrection without the cross, we will know Christ as Lord but not as Liberator of the oppressed. Christ of regal splendor is often embraced easily by the privileged as personal savior. But Christ is Priest, Prophet, Liberator, as well as King. There is always the danger that we will accept triumph based upon acceptance of the resurrection without the cross. The message is clear. The One who died on the cross is the same One who was raised from the dead.

The cross is the place of suffering and death. It is the event in which evil at its worst, including our sin and guilt, does battle with goodness at its best, including holiness and love. It represents a moral contest, even a cosmic conflict between goodness and evil. But through faith Christians see another dimension of the cross. It demonstrates "love divine, all love excelling." Nowhere else do we observe a greater love. We observe self-giving love-love poured out for the sake of us, pure *agape.* Above the agony, shame, and awesome suffering of the cross, there is an opened window through which we behold the face of God who is love.

The resurrection completes what the cross portends. It demonstrates that God has the last word. It justifies our faith in the ultimate triumph of love and goodness over all evil powers. Our path has been cut through the destruction and desolation of all evil forces. We are assured that love is stronger than hate, that death does not have a final veto over life, and that Christians need not fear separation from God through all eternity. Much more could be expressed, but in essence the center of our faith as Christians is the Easter message.

Questions for Reflection

1. Why is Easter so important to the Christian believer?
2. What is the real Easter attire? Why?
3. How are the cross and resurrection related?
4. How do you understand the importance of the cross and resurrection in depth of meaning? in relation to Christ? in relation to the Christian life?
5. How would you sum up the Easter message? Why?

Recommended Reading

Alves, Rubem, *I Believe in the Resurrection of the Body.* Philadelphia: Fortress Press, 1986.

Baillie, D.M., *God Was in Christ.* New York: The Scribner Book Companies Inc., 1948, chaps. VII ad VIII.

Chapter 19

Commentary

The Christian life is like a long journey. It is, in fact, a pilgrimage. It is like a race that does not belong to the swift. It begins with the new birth and continues everlastingly. The real test is the journey in this life with its joys and sorrows as well as its peace and temptations. It requires long-suffering and amazing patience. If it is healthy and whole, there is increasing knowledge and spiritual growth. God has made provisions for our needs. God has sent the Holy Spirit as Interpreter, Guide, Quickener, Life-Giver and Sanctifier.

One does not inherit the life of grace. We cannot assume that because we are born into a Christian family and are children of saintly parents, we are sinless. We are all sinners in a sinful environment. Those who are fortunate enough to be brought up in Christian homes have a head start. They are introduced early to the reality of sin and the availability of the grace of God. In some cases, however, a morbid, legalistic, and negative version of Christianity can drive young people in the wrong direction. The responsibility of the Christian parent is great. This is also true of pastors and teachers of the young. There is need for much study, meditation, and prayer that we may worthily communicate the words of truth and also teach by our example.

The Holy Spirit has been given to the church as well as to the individual Christian to aid us in the life of faith. The gathered, believing fellowship we know as the church was born in a mighty outpouring of the Spirit. The promise that Jesus made to his disciples to be with them was kept on the Day of Pentecost. Jesus is with the believer as well as with the fellowship of believers through the presence and power of the Holy Spirit. He is with us always.

This is great assurance, considering the nature of the life we are called to live as Christians in a world opposed to the claims of our commitment. The life we live in Christ must be lived in the world. Christians do not have the luxury of retreat from the world on a permanent basis. The Christian life is real and concrete-it is here and now. Here I speak most consciously as a Protestant theologian. If I spoke more as a Roman Catholic priest or as a Hindu pundit, I would need to modify what I have said. Thus, the emphasis here is upon how we grow in the knowledge and grace of God in this world. It has been persons such as Martin Luther King, Jr., and Dietrich Bonhoeffer who have demonstrated what this can mean. The cost and the hurt are great. We need the Holy Spirit's presence and power. We always need God's sanctifying grace. The Christian life has its joys, its rewards, its happiness, and its fulfillment. But it must never degenerate to a belief in material success and earthly prosperity. Grace is never *cheap*; it is *costly*, as Bonhoeffer says.

The distinctive role of the Holy Spirit is as agent of sanctification. Sanctification is properly viewed as a process of growth in the grace and knowledge of God. It literally refers to our being more and more like God in holiness. This is a human experience, but it depends upon divine aid. The Holy Spirit as God the Sanctifier provides the means by which Christians are led forward in the experience of sanctification.

Questions for Reflection

1. In what way is the Christian life a long journey? Describe it.
2. Is it possible to be a Christian by being born to Christian parents? Why?
3. Can you conceive of a situation where Christian piety in the home could become a negative factor for children? Reflect upon the responsibility of those who minister for youth.
4. What do we mean when we say that the church was born at Pentecost? Is the Holy Spirit central to the personal life and fellowship of Christians? Explain.

5. What does it mean to live our lives in the world as Christians? How do you understand the process of sanctification as we live a life of faith in the world?

Recommended Reading

Bonhoeffer, Dietrich, *The Cost of Discipleship*. New York: Macmillan Publishing Company, 1963.
King, Martin Luther, Jr., *Strength to Love*. Philadelphia: Fortress Press, 1981.
Pannenberg, Wolfhart, *Christian Spirituality*. Philadelphia: The Westminster Press, 1983, chap. III.

Chapter 20

Commentary

God's grace is amazing. Through divine aid the lost soul is found. Those who are estranged from God are reconciled again through grace. Christianity is not a do-it-yourself-salvation religion. There is no provision for self-salvation built into the gospel of Jesus Christ. By grace we are saved through faith as a gift from God (Ephesians 2:5-8).

Lest we be misunderstood, we hasten to add that the process of being reconciled to God includes awesome human responsibility. We work our way *from* the cross and not *to* the cross. We have already stressed that sanctification is a lifelong process. Thus, the summons is clear; we work out our salvation through great effort and tremendous odds. The temptations and struggles of the Christian life are real. Our involvement is in the context of a relation of grace with God. This is my effort, and yet it is *really* God's effort through me (Philippians 2:12-13).

Reconciliation implies separation or estrangement. But in a real sense it is the coming together of those who really belong together. We recall the often-quoted saying of St. Augustine: "Thou hast made us for Thyself, and the heart...is restless until it finds its rest in Thee." God is the creator of human life. We are unhappy and unfulfilled when we rebel against God. Our only hope for well-being as well as salvation is in returning to God. Sin has separated us from God's intention for our lives. We are never in a final sense "strangers" from God. We are "estranged." God and humans belong together, but sin has separated them. Reconciliation is the reunion of the separated, the estranged. God through Christ reconciles the world to himself (2 Corinthians 5:18-19). We are as Christians summoned to a life and ministry of reconciliation. Not only are we reconciled to God by grace, but we also become at the same time reconcilers through his grace.

Grace is available to us, but it does not work automatically. We are persons. Genuine selfhood is also a gift of God to us as humans in creation. Creation as well as redemption is God's gift. God treats us as persons in creation and gives us the gift of freedom. Along with freedom of choice, intellectual ability, and moral discernment, God lays upon us awesome responsibility-even the option of willful disobedience. It is due to our improper use of that freedom that we are separated from God by our sins. God's grace is available to aid us in restoring that lost relationship. God offers grace but does not force it upon us. Only as persons freely accept it can grace be effective in doing its reconciling work. It is true that God seeks the lost. This is the measure of divine love. But it is only as we exercise the gift of freedom and respond in repentance and faith that God's grace effects its reconciling work.

Questions for Reflection

1. Why is God's grace so amazing? What does it accomplish? Why?
2. What is our human responsibility in the experience of grace and reconciliation?

3. How does grace from God enable us to overcome estrangement and lead to reconciliation?
4. Discuss the significance of human selfhood as it relates to human response and responsibility in both creation and salvation.
5. What are the proper human responses to grace in effecting reconciliation? What is the human part? What is the divine part? How do these come together in reconciliation?

Recommended Reading

Farmer, Herbert H., *The Word of Reconciliation*. Nashville: Abingdon, 1966, pp. 1-34.
Prenter, Regin, *The Church's Faith: A Primer of Christian Beliefs*. Philadelphia: Fortress Press, 1968, pp. 147154.

Chapter 21

Commentary

The sociability of humans finds its expression in the redeemed community-the church. There are reasons why our natures as humans yearn for social expression. We naturally seek a relationship with others in all areas of life. Our expression of religious faith is not an exception. Thus the church is a proper outcome of creation and is not only an organ of redemption. Human relations, whether good or ill, are structured in societies. Human life has expressed itself in many forms, from the most elementary to very complex patterns of expression. It is not surprising, therefore, that the followers of Christ find themselves gathered in various communities of faith.

As soon as we have said how natural it is for Christians to gather in communities, we are moved to say something else. Christians are expected to go beyond what is natural. The church is more than a social gathering. It is a fellowship of those who have been redeemed by the grace of God. Christians should be aware of the justice as well as the love of God. A true fellowship of believers in Christ is not an insulated group of people divorced from the hurts and cares of the rest of humankind. It is not the gathering of people with only their "kind of people." It is not people gathered according to race, nationality, or class. It is not a male-dominated fellowship. The church is like a healthy family in which everybody is somebody. The worthiness of members of the fellowship is God-given. The dignity of each member of the fellowship can be neither given nor taken away by any human. It is God's community existing in the created order. Those who properly belong are redeemed by the same grace. This is the ground upon which they base their dignity and equality before God and with each other.

Israel of the Old Covenant was known as the People of God. This was not because the people of Israel had chosen God or that they were obedient. They were, on the contrary, chosen by God who kept his promises to Israel. It was God's faithfulness that sustained this redemptive relationship. In spite of Israel's waywardness and misunderstanding as to why it had been chosen, God's covenant-love held fast. In a similar manner the church has been referred to as the New Israel or a new Chosen People. The latter group belongs to God out of the experience of grace. Peoplehood is inclusive of all those who have received the grace of God through Jesus Christ. The fellowship transcends all racial and ethnic distinctions. Bond and free, rich and poor, male and female-all are one in Christ.

Again, even in the church we have not always understood the nature and mission of the church. We often abort the intention and mission of God's church. Most of all we do not take upon ourselves a sense of servanthood as the heart of God's salvific purpose for the church. We are painfully aware of the sins of the redeemed. The category of "redeemed sinners" aptly describes every imperfect earthly Christian fellowship, yet this would appear to be a contradiction. The church continues to be effective in the world often in spite of who we are and especially what we do or don't do. This is because God through the Spirit works through the church. We are often faithless, but God remains faithful.

The description of the real situation of our earthly pilgrimage as a Christian community need not lead to despair. It is rather a challenge to use to seek to discern what God wants to do in the world through individual Christians as well as the church, God's people. Christians are to seek a deep understanding concerning the nature and purpose of the church. It is only then that they will be able to comprehend their role and participate effectively in its ministry. Their goal is never to be successful according to the standards of the world, especially during our materialistic age. Christians are to be faithful.

Questions for Reflection

1. Relate the tendency toward sociability in humans to the reality of the Christian community.
2. In what sense does the nature of the church take us beyond the order of creation to the order of redemption?
3. Compare the church fellowship to a family. What do they have in common?
4. How does understanding God's covenant with Israel lead us to a deeper understanding of the nature and mission of the church?
5. In what sense does the mission of the church depend for its effectiveness upon our faithfulness as well as God's redemptive purpose?

Recommended Reading

Prenter, Regin, *The Church's Faith.* Philadelphia: Fortress Press, 1968, pp. 155-189.

Stewart, William, *Church.* Richmond, VA: John Knox Press, 1970, pp. 15-17.

Chapter 22

Commentary

Protestants observe two sacraments whereas the Roman Catholic Church observes seven. It is, therefore, very necessary to be diligent concerning baptism and Communion.

Beyond the particular interpretation given to Baptism by a particular denomination, there are, I believe, basic salvific meanings. Baptism has something profound to say about death to sin and resurrection to newness of life. This is the message of Easter interpreted in the rite of initiation into the Christian fellowship. It is essential that this cardinal truth of the gospel be communicated at baptism regardless of any other message, which may filter through.

Water is also an element of purification. At shrines established for worship in other religions, rites of purification by the use of water are also prevalent. This is especially true at Shinto shrines in Japan. Purity is one of the pillars of the Shinto religion, hence the custom of drinking water and washing hands at wells or fountains at the entrance of these sacred places. Baptism in a spiritual sense partakes of this implication of overcoming the defilement of pollution of sin, but seems more integral to the doctrines of sin and salvation. It is a part of corporate life and worship. Baptism is a vital initiatory ceremony that is a sign and seal of membership in the fellowship of believers. There is confession of faith expressed through this act, and there is acceptance of the new convert into the body of Christ by the members of that body.

The sacrament of Communion is a memorial feast. It is repeated frequently as a witness to Christ's death for the remission of sins. A new dimension of the benefits of Christ's death is the identification that we share with the poor and oppressed among humans. Christ's cross should help Christians bear their cross as disciples. Beyond this it should lead us to identify with those who suffer. Much suffering in the world is undeserved; it results from sinful social structures and from the pain that powerful and privileged human beings inflict upon the weak and hapless masses. Sometimes it may be based upon race or upon gender and race. There should be a direct relationship between our celebration at the Lord's Table and the doing of justice.

Questions for Reflection

1. Describe briefly your understanding of the two sacraments of Protestants.
2. How does the baptism address the saving work of God through Christ?
3. In what sense is baptism a rite of purification?
4. How do baptism and Communion relate to the Christian fellowship in worship and life?
5. Relate the celebration of Communion to the liberation of the oppressed.

Recommended Reading

Cullman, Oscar, *Baptism in the New Testament.* Philadelphia: The Westminster Press, 1950.
Hellwig, Monika K., *The Eucharist and the Hunger of the World.* Mahwah, NJ: Paulist Press, 1976.

Chapter 23

Commentary

Much has been said about various aspects of the Christian life. The life of a Christian should be informed by a serious reflection upon the entire affirmation of faith. This entire study is basic to a life of Christian discipleship.

The Christian life is a journey of faith. There are many personal, social, and psychological factors that figure in our faith development. For some there is a need to work through years of disturbing doubt to a solid faith to direct the Christian life. In a real sense each person has to take the journey. There are other pilgrims, but the journey of faith is personal. It is *my* journey.

At the same time the journey includes others. The Christian belongs to a communion of saints. The Christian life is lived amidst "a great cloud of witnesses," past and present, who embody the tenets of the faith in their lives of witness. This means that Christians have a collective witness and that there is a faith tradition.

It is essential that we be aware that the Christian life has its fulfillment. The Christian does not always live in "a veil of tears." A Christian does not invest all of her or his hopes in material things. The kingdom of God comes first. The blessedness of the kingdom is a higher happiness than that associated with earthly success. This means that the Christian has a perspective on life that leads to a different assessment of values and goals. There is a lesser love for all things of this world than the love for God. A Christian is to evaluate all things in the context of the love of God. In doing this, all things that are worthy find their rightful place in the life and relationships. These aspirations are in view as objectives. They are not a matter of possession. We are made humble by our inability to accomplish all that we hold in view as we seek to follow Christ. But we are not defeated because we see Jesus before us. It is because we know of divine direction and divine aid that we need not grow fainthearted. It is through this relationship of grace that we know peace beyond understanding.

We are becoming increasingly aware that the Christian life is not merely a personal fight against existential pain. We also do battle against the forces of injustice and the structures of evil. We often benefit from evil that causes pain to millions of other human beings. It takes due care and much social analysis and reflection to become sensitive to the web of evil in which we are entangled. The dimensions and complexity of the sin and evil often overwhelm us in our environment. Once we know what needs to be done, we can easily decide that because there is so much to be done and we are able to do little, we should do nothing. This is the case when we look at the nuclear threat, at trouble spots in our world, at the drug traffic in our country, and other problems that seem hopeless. Our faith is centered in a cross and a resurrection. Christians believe that God is able to bring life out of death. We believe that God will have the last word and that the decisive victory over evil and death has already been won. Thus, the Christian has the assurance that the contradictions of life are never final. The forces of evil are proximate, but they are never ultimate. Before the One who raises the dead, all things are possible. Our faith is in the God who controls the future.

Questions for Reflection

1. How does the entire system of Christian doctrine inform the Christian life? Illustrate.
2. Describe the Christian life as a personal journey of faith.
3. How would you describe the "communion of saints"? What is the importance of this affirmation?
4. In what sense is the Christian life an experience of fulfillment in the here and now?
5. How does the Christian life relate to structural evils? How does this modify the traditional understanding of the Christian life?

Recommended Reading

Jones, William A., Jr., *God in the Ghetto.* Elgin, IL: Progressive Baptist Publishing House, 1979.

Smith, J. Alfred, Sr., *For the Facing of This Hour.* Elgin, IL: Progressive Baptist Publishing House, 1981.

Chapter 24

Commentary

In a serious understanding of the faith, last things come first. In the face of the ultimate, all else is penultimate. The way one views the end of life and the afterlife relates to one's perspective on the present life. To view life from the vantage point of eternity changes one's angle of vision. If properly focused, this could bring eternal significance to life.

It is essential that for Christians *life* is the controlling category, rather than death. This may not appear to be so in view of the way the gospel is sometimes preached. There is something unwholesome about teaching or preaching which has little to do with improving the quality of life here and now. A deeper understanding of the Christian faith points to a different quality of life that comes from a saving relationship with God through Christ. Eternal life is the abundant life that begins with the new birth and continues in sanctification but does not end with physical death. The life we know through Christ is a life in relation to God. Because of what has happened in the resurrection, we are assured eternal life that is also everlasting.

Christians are not only sure of their personal destiny but also look forward to the rule of God. The kingdom of God is related to God's will being done. God's will is to be manifest on earth as it is in heaven. We are aware of the many obstacles to the rule of God. All around us are sins, evil, and temptations that resist the reign of God in personal and social situations. The prevalence of death and decay in our physical environment would appear to remove all grounds for belief that goodness, love, and life will triumph.

It is precisely at the point of our deepest despair that the Christian faith has a clear and decisive word of hope. Our faith does not ask us to ignore or attempt to bypass sin, evil, and death. The cross is planted solidly in the marketplace of our human order. It is in the midst of our real human situation that the cross illustrates that God has engaged the very forces of evil that we most fear and dread. A path has been cut through our "valley of the shadow of death." Truth and falsehood, love and hate, and sin and forgiveness collide in mortal conflict. The resurrection says to us that the victory belongs to God. Through faith we inherit the power that the resurrection provides. Thanks be to God who gives us the victory!

Questions for Reflection

1. What does a proper understanding of the future life bring to this life?
2. What does it mean to make life rather than death the focus of reflection on the meaning of life? Does the Christian faith emphasize life? Explain.
3. What does it mean to place emphasis upon the rule of God on earth as well as in heaven? What difference should this make for the present life?
4. When we assert that eternal life begins now for the Christian and continues everlastingly, what is involved?
5. What is the response of the Christian faith to our encounter with evil, sin, and death? Discuss.

Recommended Reading

Paul, Robert S., *Kingdom Come.* Grand Rapids: William B. Eerdmans Publishing Company, 1974.

Prenter, Regin, *The Church's Faith: A Primer of Christian Beliefs.* Philadelphia: Fortress Press, 1968, pp. 189-216.

Special Books

Theology

Lewis, C.S., *Mere Christianity.* New York: Macmillan Publishing Company, 1952.

This popular work about Christian theology is selected due to its readability as well as its ecumenical character. It is written by a lay theologian who is a literary genius. The work is well written and communicates well what Lewis views as the essence of the Christian faith. It brings the tenets of the faith home to the contemporary world.

Prenter, Regin, *The Church's Faith: A Primer of Christian Beliefs.* Philadelphia: Fortress Press, 1968.

This book is written by a systematic theologian for nontheologians. It provides a comprehensive statement of the Christian faith with the identical purpose that we have in mind in *Christian Beliefs.* I will not raise any critical points of disagreement, though there are several. We are aware that the author invites such criticism. We view the work as a vital, readable, resource. It is intended to be of ecumenical interest, and it encourages Bible study.

Bonino, Jose Miguez, *Doing Theology in a Revolutionary Situation.* Philadelphia: Fortress Press, 1975.

The selection of a text from the vast literature of liberation theology is not easy. This books is by a Protestant author who is a leader in the World Council of Churches. The book is one of the more nontechnical resources that should be a good introduction to theologies written in solidarity with those who are oppressed or those who suffer from structural evils.

Bible Resources

Anderson, Bernard W., *The Living Word of the Bible.* Philadelphia: The Westminster Press, 1979.
Anderson has brought the maturity of a lifetime of biblical scholarship to bear upon this theme which is his title. He is best known for his Old Testament study, but here he is a learned guide throughout the Bible. He has written for pastors and lay persons. We affirm his emphasis upon the living character of the Bible as well as his thematic approach to Bible study.

Goodspeed, Edgar J., *How Came the Bible?* Nashville: Abingdon Press, 1976.
In this small text is a wealth of information by a master authority on Bible languages and texts. The book is a resource with an abundance of background information that will make the Bible speak with great meaning. Few books this small are more readable or provide more information on the selected subject. This book is a rare gem!

Christ and Salvation

Baillie, D.M., *God Was in Christ.* New York: The Charles Scribner Book Companies Inc., 1948.
This remains one of the best studies of Christology in the English language. It is somewhat advanced for anyone without theological education. It is a sound and balanced study (theologically speaking), and it is presented in very readable prose. This is a classical study which is worth the study it requires to absorb its message.

McDonald, H.D., *Forgiveness and Atonement.* Grand Rapids: Baker Book House, 1984.
This is a clear, concise presentation of the Christian understanding of salvation. It is readable and biblical. In some ways

it is too simplistic and does not ask the tough questions Christians face on their pilgrimage. It is also weak on the side of moral and social responsibility.

Church, Christian Life, Ministry

Niebuhr, H. Richard, *The Purpose of the Church and Its Ministry*. New York: Harper & Row, Publishers, Inc., 1977.
This is a valuable study of the church and ministry (lay as well as clergy) by the theologian ethicist, H. Richard Niebuhr with the collaboration of Daniel Day Williams (theologian) and James M. Gustafson (ethicist). The study was written to inform those engaged in the theological education of ministers, but its content is invaluable for all persons seeking to live the Christian life and serve through the church.

Pannenberg, Wolfhart, *Christian Spirituality*. Philadelphia: The Westminster Press, 1983.
The writings of this distinguished German theologian are well-known in the English speaking world. He is generally lauded for his important contribution to political theology, but here he has provided equally valuable insights into personal spiritual development. I am impressed with the manner in which he relates personal sanctification with political involvement for a more humane social order.

Teaching Resources

Evans, Robert A. and Alive F., *Casebook for Christian Living*. Atlanta: John Knox Press, 1977.
Hestenes, Roberta, *Using the Bible in Groups*. Philadelphia: The Westminster Press, 1983.

Additional Copies of *Christian Beliefs* may be purchased by sending $15.00 plus $3.00 shipping and handling to:

The J. Deotis Roberts Press
Post Office Box 10127
Silver Spring, MD 20914

Thank you for your patronage!

Printed in the United States
By Bookmasters